# Elffolk

*and the Crystal Caves of Atlantis*

# Elffolk

## *and the Crystal Caves of Atlantis*

Tina McFadden

Small Shifts Books & Media Inc.

Small Shifts Books & Media Inc.
1446 26A St SW
Calgary, AB, T3C 1K8
Website: www.smallshifts.com



Canadian Cataloguing in Publication Data
McFadden, Tina
Elffolk and the Crystal Caves of Atlantis

ISBN: 978-1-926643-07-6 (bound) -- ISBN: 978-1-926643-03-8 (pbk)
ISBN: 978-1-926643-08-3 (e-book)

Half of the author's royalties from this book will be donated to the Fund for Youth Rights to Education Canada, a non-profit organization dedicated to enhancing the quality of, and access to, education for students around the world.

Printed and bound in China.

*For my sister Jodene*

## — PROLOGUE —

"The earth is restless," Kaya warned.

Water tumbled over black rocks and seeped into the stone floor below. The cave was dim. Gael could barely see the walls around her, let alone the spirit in the waterfall.

"Go on," Gael prompted, spotting Kaya in the falls. "You know why I'm here."

An old scroll appeared suddenly in Gael's hands. She glanced down, startled, and squinted at the symbols on the scroll.

"What am I supposed to do with this?" she asked. "You know very well I can't read."

"I'll read it," Kaya answered. "But I have to warn you, a time of great change is coming."

"Yes, yes. Just tell it to me," Gael replied." Exactly as it's written." She shut her eyes then and waited. There was a pause, and Kaya read the poem.

*The earth will shake, the mountains spew*
*A fiery molten lava stew*
*And watery walls will wash ashore*
*Erasing shorelines evermore*
*With shrinking land come desperate men*
*And war and chaos happen then*
*But those that stay a day too long*
*Will meet their end – for right or wrong*
*Forgotten then forever more*
*Somewhere beneath the ocean floor.*

Gael stumbled back a few steps, clutching the scroll to her chest. "No Kaya, it can't be. Our island – Atlantis – is to disappear into the sea?"

As if in response, the ground shook under Gael's feet. She turned towards the mouth of the cave, a frantic look on her face. But, even then, she knew it was too late. The rocks were already crashing down around her.

Through the dust and falling rock, Gael glimpsed a swirling black fog. Out of the fog, a tall, shadowy figure emerged. Instantly, the colour drained from Gael's face.

"This is your fault, isn't it?" she demanded.

The shadowy figure leaned forward in reply, outstretched one ghostly arm and took a long, deep bow.

— CHAPTER ONE —

# An Imaginary Line

It was the very last place you'd expect to find a village. There were no roads leading to it and no dot marking its place on a map. But that was precisely the way the elves wanted it. Tucked away in a valley, under the shadows of ancient pines, the village had remained a secret on the island of Atlantis for over 200 years.

Around the village, an imaginary line had been drawn. The line was an unofficial border of sorts meant to keep the elves from wandering too far. Besides, there was no particular reason to leave Elffolk. Everything an honest elf should ever need or want could be found within the village. More than that, the line had always been there, and everyone respected it.

Still, there was no accounting for the rebellious streaks of young elves.

Part-way up the mountain, Enna, a young elf, stood at the line. Being an imaginary line, there was nothing to see. So, after a lot of careful thought, she picked a spot in the forest and declared it the border.

"You had better not cross it," Nissa warned. Nissa was Enna's older sister. She stood with her arms folded across her chest, staring at Enna.

"What if I do?" Enna shrugged. "What's the worst that could happen?"

Nissa stared at her blankly. That was just it. They didn't know. Since their earliest days, they'd heard tales of the dreaded big people who lived somewhere beyond the imaginary line.

A full-grown elf reached a proud height of three feet. The big people, it was rumoured, were twice that height, and their weight was several times that of an elf. But far more frightening than their hulking size, the big people of Atlantis were said to be cold-hearted and cruel.

The truth of the matter was no elf alive in Elffolk had ever actually seen a big person. And at times, Enna half suspected that the older elves had made the whole thing up.

Enna took one giant step forward – an obvious breach of the border.

"Don't!" Nissa sucked in her breath sharply.

Enna turned and grinned. "It's an imaginary line, Nissa. It doesn't mean anything. It's just a step."

"Get back!" Nissa's hands were on her hips now, her mouth an angry thin line.

Enna glanced around, her feet planted firmly on the ground. "Seems fine, Nissa. Actually, it feels nicer over here. You should join me."

Nissa rolled her eyes and started in on a familiar lecture about rules and responsibility. As the older sister, Nissa seemed to consider it her job to keep Enna in line.

Enna turned away as her sister droned on. There was no use covering her ears. The elves didn't speak aloud to one another. They used mental telepathy to communicate – meaning they had only to think a thought and direct it at another elf. The other elf read the thought and responded with his or her own thought. They were able to communicate with animals this way as well.

Mica trotted past them both. A tall brown cat, Mica pressed on further up the mountain, well past the imaginary line. He flopped on to his side and glanced over at the elves casually. They, in turn, were gaping at him.

"What?" he asked.

"You just crossed the line!" Nissa thought. Her mouth was open and her hands were turned up in a gesture of disbelief.

"So what? I come here all the time."

"See Nissa!" Enna thought triumphantly. "It must be fine if Mica can do it...."

"I like to get away from the hustle and bustle of the village," Mica explained with a long drawn-out cat yawn.

Enna and Nissa exchanged amused glances. There was no hustle – and definitely no bustle – in Elffolk. Things moved along at a snail's pace. The elves walked slowly, strolling and sauntering from one place to the next. They took their time to eat as well, and often breakfast turned into lunch before anyone had left the table.

Mica ignored the elves' smirks. Instead, he turned his attention to his right paw, licked it a few times, and then pressed it against his ear.

Suddenly, he glanced up, his eyes wide, ears back, the fur on his head standing on end. "What was that?" He scrambled to his feet and crouched low to the ground.

Enna and Nissa froze in place instantly.

"I just heard something," Mica added.

Enna looked around through the surrounding woods. The tall evergreens cast shadows across the forest floor – shadows that now seemed very ominous. Anywhere, something – or someone – could be lurking.

"Where did the noise come from?" Nissa asked.

Mica appeared deep in thought. "You know what, on second thought, never mind. It was something else."

"What do you mean – something else?"

"It was nothing." Mica glanced away. But the elves were waiting for an explanation. "It was just my stomach growling," he added sheepishly, turning his attention to a beetle on a nearby tree. "That reminds me, I haven't had a bite to eat since breakfast."

"Mica, it was breakfast half an hour ago," Nissa retorted with a loud sigh. "Don't scare us like that."

They turned back toward the valley, winding their way through the trees. A cloud passed over the sun, and a great shadow settled over the forest like a heavy blanket.

"Wait," Mica thought. "There it is again." He stopped dead in his tracks this time. He sniffed the air and glanced up through the trees suspiciously.

"Stop it, Mica!" Nissa stomped her foot. "It's not funny."

Just then, a handful of brown birds fluttered from the tree branches. A squirrel raced down the trunk of a nearby tree and scurried past them. And a soft rustling underfoot marked the flight of mice, snakes and other small creatures tearing through the undergrowth.

Enna glanced to the sky just as a flock of yellow canaries flew past. A moment later, a second flock sailed by. They were all headed in the same direction – due south.

"Something is happening," Nissa thought worriedly. "What is it?"

"Run!" Mica's thoughts screamed out. "To the meadow!"

They sprinted through the trees at top speed, the slope of the mountain carrying them ever faster. Soon they were flying down the mountain so fast, it seemed their legs were moving on automatic, and the rest of their bodies were just trying to keep up.

Enna caught her shoulder on a rough tree trunk. She felt the sting of the scrape but pressed on. A few seconds later, she stubbed her toe on a rock. Then she heard a yelp from behind. Glancing over her shoulder, she spotted her sister. Nissa was lying face-down on the ground.

Enna tried skidding to a halt, but she couldn't slow down. Thinking fast, she wrapped her arms around a tree trunk and hung on for dear life. Her legs swung out from under her. She spun halfway around the tree. Next, she was soaring through the air. Finally, smashing into some prickly bushes, she came to a full and final stop.

Groping tree roots and branches, she clambered back up the steep slope. Nissa had rolled on to her side.

"You OK?" Enna asked, helping Nissa to her feet.

"I tripped on a tree root," she grumbled.

Mud was smeared across Nissa's cheeks. Old leaves and twigs were tangled in her blond hair. Enna could hardly believe her sister had just taken a harmless tumble. By looking at her, it would seem she had skidded halfway down the mountain on her head.

They tore off again, back down the mountain, back toward the meadow.

"Come on already!" Mica thought from somewhere ahead.

They could see the grassy meadow through the trees now. Another few seconds and they had slipped out of the forest.

Hunched over, hands on knees, they stopped to catch their breath.

"Keep running!" Mica directed. He was bounding toward the centre of the meadow. The top of his head was just barely visible above the tall grass.

They raced to the flat black boulder in the middle of the meadow, wondering whether they were being chased. When they arrived at the boulder, Mica was already standing on top. He was looking north toward the tree line, waiting, waiting for something.

"What is it?" Enna asked. She glanced around and realized they weren't alone in the meadow. A small herd of deer was resting nearby. To the west, a fox lay low in the grass and, throughout the meadow, rabbits crowded together in clusters.

Suddenly, a wild screeching sound filled the air. A black cloud erupted from the cliffs at the top of the mountain. The cloud shrank and grew and shifted shape as it approached. Enna watched with a mixture of curiosity and fear. It was like nothing she'd ever seen before. The cloud moved quickly in their direction. As it passed by overhead, she realized it was just a large group of bats.

Just then, the ground shifted under Enna's feet. She reached out, hoping to grasp something solid, but everything around her was shaking, too. The sound of crashing trees echoed through the valley. Then came the sound of tumbling rocks, smashing through the forest. The elves and animals watched, silent and still.

A few seconds passed and the shaking stopped. Enna and Nissa stood in place, wondering whether they'd felt the last of it.

"An earthquake," Nissa thought at last.

"Not like the usual little earth tremors."

"We should get back and make sure everything is all right at home."

Enna nodded, gazing into the forest. "I hope no one was hurt by all those falling rocks."

Already, the fox had slipped away. The rabbits had disappeared, too. Slowly, the other animals returned to the forest as well, to inspect the damage to their dens, warrens and nests.

As the three of them crossed the meadow and entered the woods along a well-trodden dirt path, Enna stole a glance at her sister. Nissa's knees were muddy, her hair hopelessly tangled. From the pointy tips of her ears to the pointy tips of her shoes, Nissa was downright filthy.

Enna tried to stifle a laugh, but she snorted loudly. Nissa glanced at her sister and scowled. In contrast to Nissa's dirty appearance, Enna's brown hair hung neatly around her shoulders. Her knees were clean, her shoes hardly dusty.

"It's because you're so tall and you have such long legs," Nissa thought grouchily. "I couldn't keep up."

"Oh, so it's my fault you fell?" Enna retorted. She was sensitive about her height.

At age nine, Enna was two years younger than Nissa, but a good half foot taller. When Enna stood before her grandparents, she could nearly look them straight in the eye. Already, she towered over the other youngsters in the village. And she showed no signs of slowing down. In fact, she had earned the much-unwanted nickname, *Swamp Weed.* These hardy weeds grew to the size of small trees in the swamps south of Elffolk.

They followed the winding dirt path past the "ghost village," a name they'd given the forest just west of Elffolk. Upon first glance, the area looked like any ordinary forest. However, on closer inspection, ruins could be found among the plants. Dozens of decaying homes had all but disappeared into a tangle of trees and weeds.

They hurried past the ruins, eyes focused on the path ahead. For some reason, the old, crumbling, forgotten buildings always gave them a chill. Through the trees ahead, they spotted tendrils of grey smoke rising from the stone chimneys in the village.

They passed by the community garden where an old elf named Beatle was inspecting his corn stalks for damage. He stopped what he was doing and stared at Enna, Nissa and Mica suspiciously.

"Up to no good," he thought vaguely as they passed.

Nissa rolled her eyes.

Enna was used to whispers and suspicious glances by

some of the older elves in the village. She had chalked it up to the fact that she and Nissa were being raised by their grandparents, and their grandparents didn't spend a great deal of time supervising or disciplining them.

As Enna, Nissa and Mica rounded a bend in the path, they passed by an old wooden sign. The sign stood on a steep tilt, threatening to topple right over. Thick black letters had been burnt into the wood years before, and the sign had been hammered into the ground.

Enna was told the sign read *Welcome to Elffolk,* which was ironic because there were never any visitors to welcome.

— CHAPTER TWO —

# *The Black Cliffs*

The houses in the village of Elffolk were made of mud and stone, their walls rounded, their roofs cone-shaped. Enna's grandfather was a skilled stonemason and carpenter. He had restored many of the old houses in the village.

In the village, there were two tailors, a shoemaker, a blacksmith and a baker. A family of farmers managed the wheat fields to the south. A medicine elf tended to the villagers' health and well-being.

Geter, the village chief, was responsible for organizing village meetings, celebrations and other events. He oversaw the village's day-to-day activities as well. But, most importantly, Geter made it a point to know everybody well – *especially* their business. He was a friendly chap, though, and every few days he made the rounds, stopping for tea at each elf's home.

Just before Enna and Nissa reached their front door, it swung open. Their grandmother was standing in the doorway. She collected Enna and Nissa into her arms, and promptly scolded them for not returning her thoughts. She had tried contacting them during the earthquake, but they had failed to reply.

"Sorry," Enna thought. "There was just so much going on. Is everything all right here?" Enna glanced around the small house. Bits of broken pottery littered the stone floor. A potted fern had toppled over.

"Just some plates," Grandmother replied hastily. "Let's get to the village square for any news."

They hurried along the pathway to the stairs, which led to the lower part of the village. Enna and Nissa took the steps two at a time, and this was about four times faster than any of the grown-up elves moved, even during emergencies.

Geter was already standing on a box in the centre of the village square. He was waving his arms dramatically to collect the elves' attention. A crowd had gathered around him.

"Is everyone all right?" he asked. Glancing at one another, the elves nodded uncertainly. "Any damage to the buildings?"

"A tree fell on my roof," Jasper replied. "The beams holding up the roof are damaged," he added. "And some of the stones from the walls have come loose."

Jasper was Elffolk's only middle-aged bachelor. Over the years, he had dated a number of female elves. However, he'd always found a reason to break it off – she wasn't the right astrological sign, his mother didn't approve, she didn't share his passion for pine cone collecting.... Jasper lived with his mother in the lower part of the village.

"We'll start work on your home right away," Enna's grandfather replied.

"Any other damage to report?"

"There are cracks in the walls of some of the homes, and broken trees everywhere," Seth answered eagerly, stepping to Geter's side.

Seth was Geter's right-hand elf. He was a young elf with clear political ambitions. There was no doubt in anyone's mind that Seth one day hoped to replace Geter as village chief.

Seth prided himself on his intelligence and can-do attitude. But as much as anything, he prided himself on his height. He claimed to stand a full three feet three inches tall – an admirable height for an elf. He'd been properly measured only once, though, and he refused to be measured again. Therefore, many of the elves assumed he'd been standing on his tiptoes at the time.

"It seems we got off easy, then," Geter concluded, surveying the anxious crowd around him. "Let's tend to the damage and clean up the valley. Be ready for aftershocks."

The village square began to clear as the elves returned to their homes.

"Wait!" someone called. The elves turned back to the square, glancing around in confusion. It wasn't Geter who had addressed them.

A grouchy old elf named Eiffel stepped on to the box in the centre of the square. The village hermit, Eiffel lived among the ruins of the ghost village, and he'd done so for as long as anyone could remember. He wanted no part of the village goings-on. He avoided crowds at all costs. He was rarely seen – not once bothering to make an appearance at village events. Never before had he dared to address a whole crowd of elves.

"I received an urgent message," Eiffel stated, his gaze flitting over the sea of curious faces. "It's Gael. She's trapped in the black cliffs to the north."

There were gasps among the crowd.

Gael had just celebrated her 100th birthday, which was old for an elf, but not ancient. She served as Elffolk's most senior spiritual adviser, meaning she helped the elves figure out their purpose in life and guided them along those paths. She also offered advice on personal matters and helped settle disagreements. She even advised the farmers when and where to plant their crops. But before she made any decision, she faithfully consulted the stars, the spirits and her own gut instincts.

Now, as it turned out, the elf who would have advised them on their course of action was trapped in the black cliffs.

The black cliffs stood like a fortress atop the northern mountain. They were located far beyond the imaginary line, but besides that, they were strictly off limits. It was said that a dark magic lurked within the caves of the black cliffs.

"We'll send a rescue party at once," Geter announced and pushed through the crowd.

The elves glanced at each other curiously. The rescue team would be crossing the imaginary line and entering the forbidden black cliffs. It was unheard of. Then again, no elf had ever been trapped in the black cliffs.

Within minutes, Geter had assembled his rescue team. The team included Enna's grandfather for his expertise with tools and Enna's grandmother for her keen psychic abilities. It also included the medicine elf, three of the strongest elves in the village and Geter himself.

"The rest of you, stay in the village," Geter instructed. "We'll let you know how things are coming along."

With a sinking feeling, Enna watched the rescue party leave. Nothing exciting ever happened in Elffolk. Now, for the first time in her life, there was a chance to take part in a real adventure, and she'd been left out.

"I'm sure I could help with something," Enna thought sulkily.

"Me, too," Nissa agreed. They trudged back to their house, scowls on their faces.

While Nissa scrubbed the mud from her face and plucked the twigs from her hair, Enna peered out the north-facing window of their round, one-roomed home. Tall pines blocked her view, but somewhere beyond the trees were the black cliffs.

"We could go to the black cliffs and see if they need any help," Enna suggested, still staring out the window.

Nissa eyed her warily. "We shouldn't. Geter told us to stay in the village."

"Yes, but what if they need help moving small rocks, or if they need someone to climb the cliffs? We're very good at climbing," Enna added reasonably. She could be very persuasive. Already, Enna could see the wheels turning in her older sister's mind.

"That's true," Nissa agreed. There were large rocks to the west of the village, and Enna and Nissa had spent many an afternoon climbing them.

"We could just see if they need our help. If they don't,

we could leave," Enna reasoned.

"But we'd be crossing the imaginary line, Enna," Nissa replied stubbornly.

"We'd be following the rescue team," Enna prompted hopefully.

"Yes, but it's the imaginary line! Who knows what lies beyond it?"

Enna slumped into a chair. Convincing Nissa to break a rule was no easy task. "But Nissa, we can't just sit here and do nothing!" Enna protested.

Nissa pressed her lips together, deep in thought.

"If we hurry we may be able to catch up to the rescue team," Enna added, watching her sister's face carefully.

Finally, Nissa nodded.

Alone and unsupervised, Enna and Nissa rounded the side of the house. Stealing glances toward the main path, they searched for signs of their nosy, meddlesome neighbour. If their neighbour happened to spot them on their way to the forbidden black cliffs, after they'd clearly been told to stay put, well, there would be no going anywhere for a very long time.

"Going somewhere?"

The elves froze. They turned slowly, and let out a sigh of relief. It was just Mica, sprawled across a flat rock. Eyes closed, he was soaking up rays in a warm patch of sunlight.

"We're going to the black cliffs," Nissa thought.

"I see," Mica replied with mild interest. He got to his feet slowly, lazily, as if every effort was a bit of a burden. Then, stretching his front legs before him, and his back legs behind him, he glanced up at the elves. "In that case, follow me."

With a spurt of energy, Mica tore off through the woods. He leaped over tree roots and rocks. Within seconds, he had disappeared.

"Wait up!" Enna thought.

When the elves caught up to Mica, he was resting on his haunches, plainly bored and a little put out.

"You could slow down a bit, Mica," Enna thought, panting to catch her breath.

"Or," Mica countered. "You could try keeping up. I haven't got all day, you know."

"Oh really?" Nissa asked. "What are your big plans for the day, Mica?"

Mica appeared to be thinking hard. "Well, I haven't had my lunch, as you know." He glanced up at Nissa. "After that, I have my afternoon nap. Then, before you know it, it's time to start thinking about dinner."

"Sounds like a hectic day," Nissa grinned.

"Well, some of us have to hunt for our food," he replied defensively.

"Yes, yes, I know, Mica. You lead a very demanding life."

Mica turned his head away, taking offence at the sarcasm. But Mica was a good-natured cat, and not one to hold a grudge. A moment later, his resentment had passed, and he took the lead once again, guiding Enna and Nissa up the mountain toward the black cliffs.

Suddenly, Enna stopped and looked around.

"What is it?" Nissa asked.

"I think we just passed the imaginary line."

Nissa glanced around nervously, as if the very fact that they were outside the imaginary line implied instant danger. Nissa had her reasons for being nervous. As a very young elf, she had wandered far from home and had gotten lost. A search party was sent out and a few hours later, Nissa was discovered deep in the woods – cold, disoriented and terrified. Since that day, she had never ventured too far from the village.

Enna, on the contrary, loved exploring the unknown. As they crossed the imaginary line, she felt a thrill of excitement. They were in brand new territory now. Inside the imaginary line, Enna had explored nearly every square foot of the forest. But out here, everything was new – the scenery, the trees, the soil. She smiled to herself, revelling in the adventure of it.

Yet, as they climbed higher up the mountain, the forest seemed to grow darker and the sounds of the forest faded. But Enna couldn't be sure it wasn't all just in her imagination.

And several times she could have sworn that someone was following them.

They came to a clearing in the forest and rested. The trees opened up, offering a window to their surroundings. Somewhere below was the village, but as hard as they tried, they couldn't find a single rooftop. Not a single thread of smoke rose up through the trees. Even the village square had vanished.

"It's like the whole village disappeared," Enna thought, shaking her head in disbelief.

A sudden crack, like a breaking branch, caused Enna, Nissa and Mica to turn in fright. A flash of yellow disappeared behind a tree trunk just a few yards away.

"What is it?" Enna demanded, turning to Nissa. Nissa shook her head ever so slightly, her eyes wide with fear.

A few moments passed. No one dared move a muscle! Finally, curiosity got the cat, and Mica crept toward the tree.

"Be careful!" Enna warned. She watched as Mica approached the tree, peeked around the trunk and sat down, his tail sweeping over the ground behind him.

"What is it?" Nissa asked.

"It's Ellie."

"Ellie!" Enna thought in surprise. Ellie was the daughter of their nosy, meddlesome neighbour, and clearly the apple didn't fall far from the tree, because Ellie, who was Enna's age, was just about as nosy and meddlesome as her mother.

A young elf in a bright yellow shirt emerged from her hiding place. Any shame for having been caught faded quickly, and Ellie resumed her usual smug, superior air.

"You're not supposed to be here," Ellie accused. She was much shorter than Enna, but with chin held high, she still managed to look down at her.

"Well, neither are you," Enna replied.

"Where are you going?" Ellie asked. "Think you can save Gael?"

"We're going to offer to help."

"If Geter wanted your help, he would have asked for it. You should come back now. You think just because you don't have parents, you can do whatever you want, whenever you like."

Ellie's thoughts stung Enna. It wasn't her fault she didn't have parents. Her and Nissa's parents had died when Enna was a baby. In fact, Enna had no memory of her mother or father at all. She didn't feel any sadness over her loss because she didn't know any different. Even still, she didn't need to be reminded of the fact that she was an orphan.

"We're not going back," Nissa thought firmly, her arms crossed. The colour had promptly returned to Nissa's face, and her cheeks were flushed with anger.

"Fine," Ellie replied with a shrug and turned back down the mountain. "Just don't get lost or anything. We wouldn't want to have to send out a second search party – for a *Swamp Weed*."

Nissa stared after Ellie furiously. "Unbelievable," she remarked. "Who does she think she is? And does she have nothing better to do than keep us in line?" Nissa rolled her eyes and turned away.

Enna watched Ellie as she made her way back down the mountain. Despite her irritation, Enna felt a wave of concern. Should they have left Ellie to return on her own? It was a long trek back to Elffolk, and she was far outside the imaginary line.

"We're close," Mica thought, interrupting Enna's thoughts.

They followed Mica's swishing tail up a steep, rocky incline. As they crested the hill, the trees gave way to a rocky clearing. Beyond the clearing stood an imposing rock wall. The rugged cliffs ran east along the top of the mountain for as far as the elf eye could see.

They had arrived at the black cliffs.

— CHAPTER THREE —

# *A Rescue Mission*

The sound of hammering led Enna and Nissa to Geter's rescue team. The team was facing the cliff, gathered in a semi-circle around a huge heap of loose rock.

"Enna, Nissa, what are you doing here?" their grandfather asked in surprise. His heavy hammer dropped from his hands, landing on the ground with a dull thud.

"We came to help," Enna thought quickly, hoping that the good-natured gesture might make up for the fact that they had disobeyed Geter's order.

"You rascals!"

Enna and Nissa whipped around to find their grandmother standing behind them, hands on her hips, a deep frown on her face.

"You were told to stay in the village!" she scolded.

"Yes, we know, but we thought we might be able to help," Enna thought, staring at her grandmother's feet.

Grandmother let out a long weary sigh.

"Did you find Gael?" Nissa asked quickly, hoping to change the subject.

"Not yet. Seems we have another problem." Grandfather pointed to the pile of rocks. "This was the entrance to the cave."

"Can you move the rocks?" Nissa asked.

"We've tried, but our tools just aren't enough."

"Isn't there another way in?" Enna wondered. "Couldn't someone climb over the cliff?"

"The rocks are too unsteady," Grandfather replied.

"This is the only way," Grandmother thought. Her eyes were closed and she was concentrating hard. Grandmother communicated regularly with the spirits – relatives and other souls who had passed on from this world. It appeared the spirits were guiding her now. "Yep, the only way," she repeated, nodding to herself.

Nissa crouched down next to the rubble. She was examining something. "There's a very small hole here," she thought after a minute.

Grandfather bent down and peered into the hole. "Seems to go all the way through to the cave."

"Yes, but who can fit through there?" the medicine elf asked.

"I can," Enna replied.

"I can't let you do that, Enna," Grandfather thought with a shake of his head.

"Why not?"

"It's too dangerous."

"How else will we save Gael?"

"You're too young to go alone."

Enna glanced at her sister expectantly. Nissa was staring at the hole in the rock pile, stubbornly avoiding eye contact with Enna. Discreetly, Enna poked her in the ribs. Nissa just swatted at Enna's hand.

"What are you waiting for? Offer to go with me!" Enna thought to Nissa. "That's why we're here, isn't it?"

"I'll go, too," Nissa offered reluctantly, and threw a quick, reproachful glance at Enna.

"As will I," Mica added, opening his mouth in a great yawn that revealed every last one of his teeth. "If I can keep my eyes open. Goodness, must be past my nap time."

With a hard look on his face, Grandfather weighed the options.

"Gael is growing weaker," Grandmother thought, her eyes still closed. "She's trapped under a rock."

"Let us go," Enna pleaded. "We'll hurry back. You can wait for us right here. It can't take very long."

"Gael's not close by," Grandmother thought. "These cliffs surround an open, empty space. Gael is trapped in a cave on the far side. You'll need to pass through this cave, cross the open space and find Gael in a cave on the other side. But once you pass through the rocks here, the passage is clear."

"Still, it sounds complicated," Grandfather thought. Lines of deep concern were etched into his already wrinkled face. "Will they be able to free Gael on their own?"

"I'm getting an image of a rock covering Gael's chest," Grandmother replied, moving her own hands over her chest in a circle. "It's not an overly large rock, but it's too heavy for Gael to lift herself. Enna and Nissa should be able to lift it."

"Don't forget about me," Mica thought. "I'll be there,

too. And while I make no claims of being a great weight lifter, I've certainly been able to get myself out of some sticky situations. It's not always about brawn and muscles and physical strength, you know. Sometimes, it takes strength of the mind. And that's where I excel. *The mind*."

The elves frowned at Mica. A few just shook their heads. But Mica paid no attention. He was busy licking the fur on his leg. A moment later, he had his leg behind his ear in an awkward contortion, completely forgetting the audience of elves surrounding him.

"What about the dark magic that's said to linger in these caves?" Grandfather asked.

Grandmother nodded gravely. She untied a necklace from around her neck and handed it to Enna. Dangling at the end of a long necklace was a yellow citrine crystal.

"You take this," Grandmother thought. "Remember, crystals magnify energy, so think positive thoughts."

Enna tied the necklace around her neck. She held the crystal in her hand.

"Don't focus on your fear. Focus on your goal, which is to find Gael," Grandmother added. "And as always, remember the teachings."

The teachings – Grandmother had recited the teachings to Enna so many times, they were practically branded in her brain. The teachings were as old as time, according to Grandmother, and there were a great many of them. However, the very first was the most important.

The first teaching was the Law of One. This law stated that there is only Oneness – one source, one energy that connects all beings and all things. It can never be broken or taken away, and you always remain a part of it. Wherever you go, there it is.

They were followers of the Law of One, Grandmother said. That meant they were followers of the old way. Enna wondered whether there could be followers of anything else.

"All right, you can go," Grandfather thought with a heavy sigh. "But be careful, and stay in touch with me and your grandmother at all times."

Enna nodded, putting on her bravest face. She was ready for the challenge, but she couldn't help but feel nervous. They were heading into the mysterious caves of the black cliffs without a guide, without a map, and they were entirely on their own. Enna had asked for adventure and she'd been given just that. Still, she wondered whether she was ready for it.

"Take my pack," Grandfather thought, setting it on the ground. "There's a canteen of water, dried bread and fruit, some matches, a lantern and a blanket."

Mica poked his head into the pack and rummaged around. He reappeared a few seconds later, looking disappointed with his findings.

"I'll have to meet you back here," he thought.

"Where are you going?" Enna asked.

"To the village – for provisions." With that, he tore off through the woods.

"Provisions?" Enna wondered.

"Supplies for the journey," Nissa answered dryly. "In Mica's case, that'll be food."

Grandfather just shrugged. "I guess it's just the two

of you then." He forced a smile. The edges of his mouth lifted, but there was no twinkle in his eye. "Go find Gael and bring her back to us."

"We will," Enna replied with forced confidence.

"Be careful crawling through that hole," Grandfather advised. "You mustn't disturb the rocks around you. The whole pile of rocks is very unstable."

Enna glanced at her older sister, wondering whether she might offer to take the lead. She was the older sister, after all. But Nissa's arms were folded across her chest and she had a deep frown on her face. Crawling through a hole in a pile of rubble appeared to be the very last thing Nissa wanted to do.

"I'll go first," Enna offered.

Nissa nodded at her. "You should be fine," she thought unconvincingly.

Any last shreds of courage drained from Enna's body. "Yeah, thanks a lot," she thought sarcastically.

The rescue team watched silently as Enna approached the cliff. With a deep breath, Enna lowered herself to the ground. She peered into the tunnel and realized she would have to wiggle her way through the small space like an earthworm. She couldn't tell how far the tunnel went. About a foot in, everything went black.

She pushed the pack ahead of her and wriggled her way through the narrow opening. Part-way through the tunnel, a feeling of panic swept over her. She had always hated small spaces.

*What if I get stuck?* she wondered to herself. Squeezing her eyes shut, she tried to imagine herself somewhere else, anywhere else. *I'm back in the meadow, lying on the black rock, enjoying the sun. I'm sitting on my front porch in the old rocking chair made of twisted tree branches.*

"Keep on going," Grandfather instructed, interrupting Enna's thoughts. Enna opened her eyes and returned to reality.

*You can do this,* Enna thought to herself. With a burst of determination, she wormed her way through to the end of the tunnel.

She clambered to her feet, stumbling in the darkness. With arms outstretched, she felt the cold rock walls. The cave was spacious – nearly six feet tall with lots of room to move around.

"I made it," she informed the others. "I'm inside the cave. I can stand right up. Actually, it's quite roomy in here."

She pulled the lantern from the pack and lit it with a match. *It's not so bad,* Enna thought, glancing at the black rock walls around her. Yet, even as she thought it, an uneasy feeling overcame her.

A keen sixth sense was common among the elves. They relied heavily on their intuition – a feeling or knowing that couldn't be explained by any of the other five senses. They were very aware of their surroundings and could often detect the presence of something, or someone, before they could see it.

There was a presence lingering in the caves – that was certain. What it was exactly, Enna couldn't be sure.

A minute later, Nissa emerged from the tunnel.

"You elves all right?" Grandfather asked.

"Yep, we made it," Enna replied quickly.

"Good work. Now, you'll just follow the cave, and –"

"Yes, we know."

Enna brushed the dirt from her shirt and shorts. She looked at Nissa. Once again, her older sister was covered in dirt, even managing to begrime her cheeks and nose.

Slinging Grandfather's pack over her shoulder, Enna stepped deeper into the cave. The temperature was cool, and she found herself shivering. Holding the lantern at arm's length ahead of her, she peered into the cave. The cave continued, widening and narrowing in places, and then turned a sharp corner.

"Do you think we should wait for Mica?" Enna asked. "Where is he, anyway?"

"He probably got distracted by a mouse," Nissa replied with a sigh. Mica was always getting distracted, and generally his distractions involved food.

"Or, maybe he's planning to join us after his afternoon nap," Enna added. That was the other thing – Mica sure enjoyed a good nap. And if he didn't get it, he was unapologetically cranky.

"Let's just go," Nissa thought. "Mica will catch up to us, if he wants to." She waited for Enna to lead the way through the cave.

It wasn't long before they heard the pitter-patter of soft paws on the rock floor behind them. Mica appeared, bulging bags of food dangling at his sides. The bags were tied around his waist like some kind of saddle.

"What's in there?" Nissa asked.

"Various cat treats – for the road," Mica replied.

"Oh Mica, you look ridiculous," Enna thought. Both Enna and Nissa burst into fits of laughter.

"That's fine," Mica replied, holding up his head proudly. "A cat's got to eat. You can't have a half-starved cat guiding you."

"Mica, when have you ever been half starved?" Enna asked, shaking her head. "Anyway, we don't need you to guide us. It's not like you've been in these caves."

Mica stopped in his tracks and looked genuinely confused. "But I'm always the lead."

"Fine, go ahead," Enna thought with a shrug and motioned for him to pass. "We know where we're going, anyway. We just have to follow this cave, cross some sort of open space, and then find Gael in a cave on the far side. By the way, where did you get all the food – and that ridiculous saddle?"

"It's not a saddle," Mica retorted. "Your neighbour gave it to me. Oh, and she's not too happy about this adventure of yours."

"Ellie must have tattled on us," Nissa thought in a huff.

"No, Ellie hadn't returned yet," Mica replied. "I was the one who told her."

"Well, it's not an adventure, anyway," Enna corrected. "It's a rescue mission."

"Potato, potahto," Mica replied coolly, and brushed past her.

— CHAPTER FOUR —

# *Something Lurks in the Shadows*

The cave wound this way and that. At times, the passage was so narrow, the elves were forced to turn sideways to slip through. At other times, it opened up to the size of a large room. The second time the cave opened up, Nissa glanced around, inspecting the area carefully. She found a few small rocks on the ground, along with footprints in the dirt.

"We're back at the beginning," Nissa thought. "Can you believe it? We've been walking in a giant circle!"

"Or, maybe we've walked it more than once," Enna added, feeling discouraged. They'd been gone a long time – and they hadn't gotten anywhere.

"Well, time for a snack," Mica decided. He circled the ground a few times before finding a suitable resting spot. "Now if you could just get me some of those dried snacks on the left." He turned his head, sniffing the bag of cat treats.

Enna untied the bundle and handed Mica a few pieces of dried – whatever they were. Frankly, she'd rather not know.

"What's the problem?" Grandmother asked, entering Enna's thoughts.

"We're back at the start! We've been walking in circles."

There was a long pause, and finally Grandmother replied, "Somewhere along the tunnel, there will be a passage to your left. This passage will lead you in the right direction. I can't tell you where it is – only to keep your eyes open. It's easy to miss."

Enna relayed the message to Nissa, who breathed out a heavy, exasperated sigh. "She doesn't know where it is?"

"No. I guess we'll just have to be more observant."

"What a gigantic waste of time," Mica thought, gobbling his cat treats and not bothering to look up. "I should have just waited for you right here and saved myself the effort."

"We should get going," Nissa thought as Mica polished off the last of his snacks. "This place gives me the creeps."

"Shall I join you this time?" Mica wondered, his tail flicking playfully. "Or, wait until you come around the next time?"

"Just keep your eyes peeled," Enna thought. "Remember, it's a passage on the left."

Enna, Nissa and Mica trudged onward, ducking under low-hanging rocks, squeezing through narrow parts. Enna ran her hand along the wall as she shuffled through the cave. Nissa stopped every few feet to inspect the wall to her left, searching high and low for the elusive passageway.

They had wasted another half hour, and still they were no further ahead. With a frustrated sigh, Nissa sat down, leaned back against the wall, and disappeared!

A loud scream pierced the caves as Nissa slid head-first down a smooth, sloping tunnel. A few seconds later, she landed with a thud.

"I found the passage," she thought weakly.

Enna and Mica raced into the tunnel after Nissa. Immediately, Enna lost her footing and crashed on to her bottom. The sloping tunnel carried her another few feet. Next, she was tumbling through the air. She landed in a tangled heap next to Nissa.

Mica, who had maintained his footing, balanced at the end of the slide and overlooked the scene. With a graceful leap, he soared past both Enna and Nissa, landing on the smooth rock behind them. He turned, sat down and wrapped his tail around himself neatly.

Enna and Nissa clambered to their feet, inspecting the damage to their arms and legs. No broken bones, no smashed heads, no gushing wounds. Just scrapes and a few bruises.

"That was fun," Nissa thought dully, collecting the lantern from the ground. By some miracle the glass in the lantern hadn't broken, and the wick was still burning. They glanced around and realized they were standing in a large, circular chamber.

Long, pointed stalactites hung from the cave ceiling like icicles, water dripping from their sharp ends. A pool of water had collected in the centre of the cave floor, and it was slowly seeping into cracks in the rock. Below there was the sound of rushing water – an underground river.

Mica glanced up to the ceiling of the chamber. "You sure wouldn't want one of those pointy things falling on you," he commented.

"Where are we supposed to go from here?" Nissa wondered.

Enna searched the chamber walls. There were no visible passageways leading out. The tunnel seemed to end there.

"There's got to be a way out," Enna thought, crossing to the other side of the chamber. "It can't just end here!"

A sudden crashing sound caused Enna and Nissa to turn in alarm. A long stalactite lay shattered on the ground, inches from Mica.

The elves rushed to Mica's side.

"That was close," Mica thought, still shaken. "It just missed me."

Enna wrapped her arms around Mica and hugged him.

"OK, OK, not too tight," Mica replied, backing away. "I just ate, you know."

"Oh, Mica," Enna thought fondly. "You've always just eaten."

"Well, there's nothing wrong with a healthy appetite," he replied, purring.

"Let's get out of here," Nissa thought, glancing at the stalactites overhead. "Maybe the earthquake loosened some of those things. Help me find a way out."

They walked around the chamber, feeling their way along the rock walls as they went.

"Up there!" Nissa thought, pointing to a hole in the wall about six feet above the ground. She turned to Enna expectantly.

"It's your turn to go first," Enna thought.

"Fine," Nissa replied with an annoyed sigh.

Enna watched her sister scale the wall like a spider. Digging the tips of her toes into cracks and holding on to bumps with the ends of her fingers, Nissa climbed quickly. With one final stretch of her arm, she gripped the top of the wall. She pulled herself up and over the edge.

"It looks like some kind of tunnel," Nissa confirmed.

Enna shuddered at the thought of another tunnel. The last tunnel had nearly done her in. How could she face another one?

"Well, go investigate," Enna thought to Nissa. "Find out whether the tunnel actually leads somewhere before we all climb up there."

"I'm not going in there by myself," Nissa scoffed. She held out her arms. "Toss me the pack and lantern."

Standing on the tips of her toes, Enna threw the pack and lantern to Nissa. Then she examined the rock wall before her.

Forcing the toes of her right foot into a crevice in the rock, Enna pushed up. Stretching her left arm as far as she could, she grasped a bump in the rock. She felt her fingers slipping and quickly stuck her left foot in a tiny hole further up the wall. She pushed up again, her right arm reaching. Nissa grabbed her wrist and pulled her into the tunnel.

"OK, Mica. Your turn."

Mica backed up. Resting his weight on his hind legs, he sprang from the ground. His front paws cleared the wall, and with the aid of his back claws he pushed up over the edge.

The elves stared into the dark tunnel before them.

"See, it's pitch dark in there," Nissa thought defensively. "Who knows what's in there?"

Mica pushed past them into the tunnel. He turned around, his yellow eyes glowing in the dark. "Coming?"

The tunnel was just high enough that Enna and Nissa could crawl on their hands and knees.

Enna put out the lantern and dropped it into her pack. There was no way she could crawl and still carry the lantern in one hand.

"It's so unbelievably dark in here," Nissa commented tensely.

"It can't be much further," Enna thought. *Or can it?* she wondered to herself. They were wandering the caves of the black cliffs, after all. Who knew what kind of frightful things awaited them – endless dark tunnels being at the top of Enna's most frightful list.

Enna tried hard to concentrate on the teachings. *Don't focus on your fear. Focus on your goal.* She breathed deeply – a trick Grandmother had taught her, and she felt the fear melt away just a little.

"This is the longest tunnel in the world. When does it end? You know, something could live in these caves. I mean, it's likely *something* lives here," Nissa rambled.

"Will you stop it?" Enna snapped. "It's not helpful."

They crawled on in silence, the rough tunnel floor wearing at their hands and knees, scraping their skin.

Mica stopped abruptly, causing Nissa to bump into him.

"What are you doing?" she asked impatiently. "We have to keep moving, Mica."

"Well, I don't want to raise any alarms," he thought gingerly. "It's just that I thought I heard something behind us."

"Yeah, it was probably your stomach growling for more food," Enna thought. "It *has* been fifteen minutes since you last ate."

"Wait," Nissa thought. "I just heard something, too."

They listened for further noises, but there was nothing. Just a dull, eerie silence.

"What did you hear?" Enna asked a few seconds later.

"It sounded like some kind of scraping," Nissa thought nervously. "Like nails, or claws scratching on the rock behind us."

"And breathing," Mica added. "A creepy, wheezy kind of breathing."

"It's probably all in our heads. I mean, it could be Mica's claws and our own breathing echoing through the tunnel," Enna suggested lightly. She was trying to stay cool, calm and collected. For goodness sake, someone had to. However, despite her outward calmness, there was an uncomfortable lump in her throat like she'd just swallowed a bunch of cooked potato without properly chewing it. "Let's just keep going."

Eventually, the tunnel emptied into a large cavern. Lighting the lantern, Enna glanced up, searching the ceiling for stalactites. There were none.

The lantern light danced across the walls in reflection. Curiously, Enna moved closer to the walls. They were smooth to the touch. She turned in a circle. All around them were massive white crystals, standing on end like giant glass columns.

*Crystal caves,* Enna thought to herself.

"Wow!" Nissa thought, turning on the spot to examine the cave from all angles. She was clearly impressed, and it took a lot to impress Nissa. "Grandmother would love this."

Grandmother was an avid collector of crystals. Much to Grandfather's displeasure, their house held a very large collection of stones and crystals. In fact, the rocks took up a good chunk of the living space. A few years ago, the rocks had grown so numerous, they had forced Grandfather's favourite rocking chair out on to the front porch. Grandmother often threatened that soon the rocks would take over Grandfather's side of the bed, and he'd be forced to sleep on the porch as well.

Each type of crystal had its own unique powers. Some had healing abilities. Others helped clear the mind or improve the memory. Grandmother spent long hours communing with her rocks of various shapes and colours. She had white quartz and clear crystals. She had yellow citrine, rose quartz and purple amethyst. But most treasured of all was her black crystal that she kept under lock and key. She called it her Stone of Truth.

It wasn't just Grandmother who believed in the benefits of crystals. All of the elves kept crystals in their homes. The medicine elf even used them in his healing practice. Grandmother, though, was the most enthusiastic collector.

The match that Enna had used to light the lantern burned down to her fingers, and she dropped it to the ground. The flame flickered one last time in final farewell and took its leave in a smoky puff.

A scratching noise echoed through the tunnel. This time it was unmistakable. Enna and Nissa stared at each other, eyes wide.

"What do you think that was?" Nissa asked, her body as still as the crystals around her.

"I have no idea."

"I could investigate," Mica offered.

"No, let's stay together," Nissa thought.

They moved on, Mica leading the way through the cave. He had picked up the pace so Enna and Nissa were practically jogging to keep up. However, there were no objections this time. Now, more than ever, they were all eager to get outside and into the sunlight.

Just then, a cold hand seized Enna's arm. She gasped in fright.

"It's just me," Nissa thought.

"Why did you do that?"

"I just saw something."

"What?"

"I don't know, but I turned around, and there were two glowing green eyes. Whatever it was sank back against the rock and into the shadows. But I'm telling you, something is following us."

Enna swallowed hard. Her heart was pounding in her chest like a mad drummer.

"There's no point being attacked from behind," Mica thought grimly after a minute had passed. "I'll go back to check it out."

"I'll go, too," Enna added.

"You're leaving me?" Nissa asked anxiously.

"We'll be back soon," Enna replied, motioning for Nissa to stay behind. But Nissa, who was frozen with fear, was clearly not going anywhere, anyway.

Enna and Mica retraced their steps through the cave. Enna was glad to have Mica at her side. She knew he could hold his own in battle with his razor-sharp claws and teeth. He'd had encounters with animals in the woods – the odd cat or fox, and one unpleasant run-in with a wild pig. But each time Mica had emerged victorious – even if he was missing a chunk of fur.

"Do you see anything?" Nissa wondered nervously from behind them. "Don't be too long, OK?"

"Nothing yet," Enna answered.

Enna and Mica entered the crystal cavern and glanced around. Their eyes swept the cavern, side to side, up and down. It was empty. Whoever – or whatever – had been following them was gone now.

They returned to find Nissa crouched low on the ground. She was watching warily in both directions.

"Nothing," Enna thought.

"There was something there," Nissa insisted.

"I believe you."

"I wish we were back in our meadow," Nissa thought longingly, as they continued through the cave.

"With lots of large, juicy rodents," Mica added.

Both Enna and Nissa frowned at him.

"Well, since we were making wishes...."

They trudged onward, the lantern lighting up the cave just a few yards ahead of them. Then, all of a sudden, the cave simply stopped.

They stared a long time at the rock wall, as if they didn't quite believe their eyes. After all this time, they had arrived at a dead end.

"It can't be," Nissa thought. "It can't just end here. There has to be a way out of this place!"

Both Enna and Nissa felt the wall, frantically searching for hidden passageways.

"Maybe we took a wrong turn," Mica thought.

"But there were no other turns to take!" Nissa argued.

Enna stared at the wall again, a wild look on her face. It was dark, cold and cramped in the caves – not to mention that they had a creepy cave dweller following them. Now, on top of it all, they were trapped. Desperately, Enna ran her hands along the wall, willing it to open up.

"Here!" Nissa thought. "There's a crack in the wall. It's not very wide, but we should be able to slip through."

A jagged, narrow opening extended from the floor to the ceiling like a large tear in the black rock.

"You first, Mica," Nissa instructed.

Mica slipped into the crack, his tail waving one last time before disappearing. Turning sideways, Nissa followed and vanished from sight.

An uneasy feeling was welling inside Enna as she stood alone in the cave. It was her turn to squeeze into yet another small space. She took a deep breath and stared at the crack, wishing it would widen just a little.

Suddenly, she glanced back into the cave. She hadn't seen a thing, but she had felt it. Something was approaching.

The lantern flickered at Enna's feet, casting a warm

glow several yards around her. Beyond that the light faded quickly into blackness.

"Who's there?" Enna demanded into the blackness. "Show yourself."

Out of thin air, a wispy black fog began to swirl. Frozen with fear, Enna watched as the fog churned and grew. It was forming into something. Already, Enna could see the outline of a head and shoulders.

Without further delay, Enna clutched the handle of the lantern. Exhaling, she squeezed into the narrow crack in the rock. She tried to ignore her fear of small spaces as she shuffled along sideways. "How much further?" she wondered. She didn't dare look behind her in case the black fog had followed.

She continued to shuffle along sideways a few inches at a time. It seemed the cave walls were closing in. Beads of sweat formed on her brow. Her breathing grew shallow. "How much further?" she asked again. Panic was setting in.

"Just a bit further," Nissa replied.

The crack widened ever so slightly as Enna rounded a corner. All of a sudden, she was facing a blinding bright light. She held up a hand to shield her eyes.

"What is that light?"

"It's the sun, Enna!" Nissa laughed. "You remember the sun?"

— CHAPTER FIVE —

# *A Quicksand Bath*

Before Enna could see anything, she felt long grasses tickling her legs. It took a moment for her eyes to adjust to the bright sunlight.

Enna, Nissa and Mica were standing at the edge of a grassy meadow, surrounded by tall black cliffs. Embedded into the cliffs were hundreds – make that thousands – of crystals of different shapes and sizes. Large, six-sided crystals jutted from the rock at odd angles. Clusters of tiny crystals covered other sections of the cliffs. Some of the crystals were completely clear, others a milky white.

The crystals caught and reflected the light, dancing in the sun like diamonds.

Even under their feet, crystals poked through the soil. A *crystal garden,* Enna thought, gazing across the field. She scooped up a loose crystal from the ground and placed it in her pack. She'd bring it home to Grandmother.

"There was something back there," Enna thought.

"What was back there?" Nissa demanded, all colour draining from her face. "That thing I saw?"

"No, it was something else. I have no idea what it was," Enna answered truthfully. "Some kind of black fog."

Never before had she seen anything like the black fog. She'd encountered plenty of spirits in her life, but this was different. The black fog's presence was darker and heavier. It wasn't anything she ever wanted to see again.

"Well, let's not wait around for it," Nissa thought.

"Want to know what I think?" Mica asked. Enna and Nissa turned to look at him. He flopped on to his side and yawned. "I think it's time for a nap."

Enna gave Mica an exasperated look. "Gael's lying in a cave somewhere, a rock on her chest, and she needs us to save her! You stay here and take a nap, if you must, but we have to find her."

"Don't mind if I do," Mica replied. He closed his eyes, content under the sun's warm rays, and rested his chin on an outstretched leg.

As Enna and Nissa crossed the meadow, they got a good look at themselves and at each other. Their knees were scraped and bloody, their fingernails black, and they were filthy – head-to-toe filthy.

"You could sure use a bath," Nissa commented, eyeing her sister with disapproval.

"Speak for yourself," Enna thought. "You were filthy even before you stepped into the caves."

Nissa tried combing her hair with her fingers, but there was no point. Her hair was horribly and hopelessly tangled. Pouting, she glanced back at Enna. "Yeah, well, you have pieces of black rock in your hair!"

Cringing, Enna shook her head. Sure enough, tiny pieces of black rock tumbled from her head.

Nissa grinned. She knew how much Enna hated to get dirty.

They pressed on, and Enna made it a point not to look at her sister at all. A minute later, Enna realized Nissa wasn't with her anymore. Where had she gone? Scanning the meadow, she spotted Nissa bent over in the tall grasses. She was staring at something.

Enna joined her sister and stared, too. Before them, in the middle of the meadow, was an oasis. Rough black rocks and smooth white crystals surrounded a beautiful pool of water – the clearest, purest spring water they'd ever laid eyes on. At least twenty feet across, the pool appeared to be quite deep in the centre.

"Do you think it's real?" Nissa asked.

"What do you mean? Why wouldn't it be?"

Nissa shrugged. "In that case, I guess this is your lucky day."

They kicked off their shoes and dipped their toes in the water. Finding the water cool, but not cold, they plunged into the pool, clothes and all.

Enna floated on her back, staring up at the azure sky, while Nissa swam in small circles beside her. There was a small pond just outside of Elffolk. During the warm summer months, they spent many hours in the water.

"Do you think we should have come in here?" Nissa asked after a few minutes. She was treading water, her arms floating at her sides.

"Why not?"

"Doesn't it seem too good to be true?"

Just like that, the water grew dark and murky. Within seconds, it had transformed into the colour of mud. The elves were no longer buoyant in the water. The liquid had become heavy, and it was dragging them down. All at once, they realized they had waded into a pool of quicksand.

Enna reached for the nearest rock at the edge of the pool, but she was a few inches too short. Her movements only caused her to sink further into the sludge.

"I told you it was too good to be true!" Nissa thought. She was struggling to swim to the edge of the pool, but she wasn't getting any closer. The mud was taking her in only one direction – down.

"Stop squirming," Enna thought.

Nissa twisted her head toward Enna, an expression of pure panic on her face. "What?"

"Stop moving, or you'll sink!"

"I'm sinking anyway!"

"Don't panic," Enna thought, though she was on the verge of panic herself.

"Call for Mica," Nissa thought desperately as the sand reached the top of her neck.

"Mica!" Enna called in thought. "Mica, help us! We're going to drown!"

A minute passed, and there was no sign of Mica.

"Mica!" Enna tried again. "Get your furry butt over here!"

Two pointed ears appeared over a black rock at the edge of the pool. Then Mica's full face came into view. He stared at the elves in disbelief, not sure what to make of the scene. Enna and Nissa appeared as two disembodied heads floating on the mud.

"What have you two gotten yourselves into?"

"We were taking a bath," Enna answered.

"Bathing in mud? What a ridiculous idea."

"Never mind. Just save us. Find something to pull us out with."

Mica disappeared into the tall grasses.

"See if you can find a long branch or something," Enna directed. "Maybe a few thick pieces of grass…."

"How about a rope?" Mica asked, returning with a rope in his mouth. How he had managed to find a rope in a meadow in the middle of nowhere was anyone's guess.

"Toss it to me," Enna thought quickly. Already, the mud had reached Nissa's chin, and it was approaching the top of her own neck.

"All right," Mica thought doubtfully. He stepped to the pool's edge. Glancing down, he paced back and forth a few times, wary of the mud.

"You can't throw it to us from there," Enna thought. "You'll have to take a few steps into the mud. It's shallow there."

Mica eyed Enna, the mud, then Enna. He looked even more skeptical. He hated getting wet – getting muddy was even worse. Delicately, he dipped a paw into the mud, and shrank back in disgust, shaking the offending paw. He paced a bit more along the edge, then very reluctantly, dipped his paw into the mud once again.

"Come on, Mica!" Enna thought. "We're sinking!"

"I need a minute," Mica thought, clearly stressed.

"We don't have time for you to mull things over!" Enna thought frantically. Nissa's bottom lip was covered in mud. She was perfectly still now, her eyes closed, as if she had already accepted her terrible fate.

Willing himself to take the plunge, Mica stepped into the shallow end of the pool. He threw back his head and tossed the rope to Enna. It came up short. There was no way she could reach it.

With disgust, Mica grasped the now muddy rope between his teeth, and stepped further into the pool. He shuddered as the mud closed in around the tops of his legs. With a toss of his head, he let go of the rope once more.

Enna stretched her arm through the mud toward the rope. It was like moving in slow motion. It took all of her strength and all of her might to push through the thick sludge. Already, the rope was disappearing into the mud.

She imagined her hand grasping the end of the rope. As she reached for it, she felt the frayed end of the rope through the mud, and clung to it with the tips of her fingers. Slowly, she pulled the rope toward her and passed it to Nissa.

"Do you see the rope?" Enna asked her.

"No," Nissa replied, refusing to open her eyes.

"It's right in front of you. Just lift your hand through the mud and hang on."

Nissa followed the instructions. Her mouth was covered in mud, her nostrils flaring in and out with each breath. A few seconds passed, and a small, dirty hand emerged from the sludge. Clenched in Nissa's hand was the rope.

"Now pull, Mica!" Enna directed.

Happy to retreat from the mud, Mica backed up, the end of the rope tight between his teeth. Slowly, Nissa began to move, sliding through the slippery sludge.

Nissa reached the edge of the pool and stumbled out. Dripping with mud, she tossed the rope back into the pool. Enna caught the rope and hung on for dear life.

The consistency of the pool was changing again. The mud was hardening around Enna. She could barely move her toes, and her legs seemed stuck in place. Soon she'd be encased in the mud.

Despite Nissa's best efforts, Enna's body refused to budge.

"Heave!" Mica directed from the side of the pool. "Heave Nissa! Heave!"

Nissa pulled harder, leaning back, using all of her weight to haul her sister out.

"Heave! Heave!" Mica ordered. "Come on, Nissa! Put some muscle into it! This isn't a friendly game of tug of war, you know."

Nissa glared at him, her face beet red from the strain. "Instead of supervising from over there, why don't you help me?"

"I suppose I could do that," Mica realized. Biting down on the rope just ahead of Nissa, Mica added his muscle to the effort.

Enna shifted in the hard mud, and then, ever so slowly, she eased forward.

"It's working!" Nissa thought excitedly. The mud was loosening its grip. Together, Nissa and Mica pulled as hard as they could, and Enna slid out.

Both Enna and Nissa collapsed on to the grass beside the pool.

"What just happened?" Grandmother demanded, sensing the danger. Enna explained how they had escaped the quicksand, and Grandmother expressed her relief. Following that, Grandmother warned them to be careful, and to remember the teachings. "Don't forget, if you need help, you can call upon the spirits," she added.

Mica eyed the elves up and down. They were coated in thick brown mud. It caked their necks, arms and legs, and it weighed down their clothes. In the warm sun, the mud was quickly drying and cracking.

"Good thing you took a bath," Mica thought. "Big improvement."

"It was clear water when we went in. We're not totally crazy," Enna replied. "Anyway, thanks for saving us." She turned to Mica and smiled wryly. "Sorry to interrupt your nap."

"No need for thanks," Mica replied, purring. "Besides, I wasn't napping."

"What were you doing?"

"Chasing rats."

"So, there are rats here, too?" Nissa demanded, glancing nervously into the tall grass around her. "Well, it just gets better and better. What is this place – your worst nightmare?"

"The largest, plumpest rats I've ever laid eyes on," Mica replied, ignoring Nissa's comments, still expecting the elves to share in his joy and wonderment. "Just fabulous feasting. Just fabulous."

"Wow, that's great, Mica," Nissa replied sarcastically. "A creepy cave creature, pools of quicksand and monster rodents. Come to think of it, didn't you wish for a meadow full of large, juicy rodents?"

"Indeed," Mica answered happily.

Enna glanced at her sister. Hunched over in the tall grass, coated in dried mud, Nissa looked like a rock statue. Enna recalled the terrified expression on Nissa's face when the mud had reached her lips. She remembered her own fear, and pulled Nissa into a hug.

"I'm glad you're OK," Enna thought.

"I really thought that was it," Nissa replied.

"I didn't," Enna declared. "I knew we'd get out."

"As much as I, too, enjoy these touching family moments, isn't there an elf that needs saving?" Mica asked. He was busy licking the last of the mud from his legs. "Something about a rescue mission.... Something about an elderly elf trapped under a heavy rock...."

"All right, Mica," Enna thought with a sigh. She pulled Nissa to her feet, and they pushed on in silence.

## — CHAPTER SIX —

# *Fowl Play*

The dried mud was tugging at their hair and stretching their clothes. Enna and Nissa didn't dare look at each other – they only reflected each other's dirty appearance. They were exhausted from their adventure in the pool. It wasn't every day that one escaped death so narrowly. Each step they took felt heavy and strained, and they longed to rest.

"OK, call me crazy, but it seems like the black cliffs are moving backwards," Nissa remarked. Enna and Mica glanced up. Sure enough, the cliffs loomed in the distance, and they didn't seem to be getting any closer.

They walked three abreast through the meadow. Twice Enna tripped over crystals poking through the ground. She was in a foul mood. Nothing was going right. It had taken them ages to find their way out of the caves, they couldn't tell quicksand from clear water, and now she couldn't even walk without tripping. Oh yeah, and she was covered in mud like a filthy worm.

A minute later, Enna stopped walking, her arms hanging heavily at her side. Nissa and Mica turned to her curiously.

Enna just pointed to the black cliffs ahead. They weren't getting any closer. If anything, the cliffs were growing smaller, more distant.

"What's wrong with this place?" Nissa asked, glancing around the meadow suspiciously. Fear settled over her like a cold shadow.

"It's the dark magic," Enna surmised, and an eerie mood overtook them all. She clutched Grandmother's crystal pendant in her palm, and tried to think positive thoughts.

"Why don't we grab a bite to eat, and then maybe things will seem better," Mica suggested. As far as he was concerned, food always changed things for the better.

"That's not a bad idea," Enna replied, realizing her hunger. "I could use a snack."

"Fine," Nissa sighed. "It's not like we're making any progress anyway. I wish Grandmother could have been a little more specific about where we're going."

They wandered to a flat black boulder, and Enna released her pack from her tired shoulders. She emptied the contents of the pack, and Nissa sifted through the bread sticks and dried fruit.

Enna untied Mica's bag and grabbed three cat treats.

"A few more," Mica thought, glancing at Enna's hand. "Saving lives works up quite an appetite."

Enna dipped into Mica's bag once more, and dropped a handful of cat treats in front of him. He purred in satisfaction, giving the treats a once-over inspection with his nose.

"I have a weird question," Nissa thought, chewing on

a piece of dried fruit. "Does this place seem anything like our meadow?"

Enna glanced around. She had to agree, there were some striking similarities between the two places: tall grass, for one; a flat black boulder in the middle, for two. Also both places looked about the same size. Of course, there was one major difference. Pine trees surrounded their meadow back home. Here, they were surrounded by cliffs and countless crystals.

"Probably just a coincidence," Enna thought dismissively, finishing off the last of their snacks.

"Help me!"

Enna, Nissa and Mica glanced at one another in surprise.

"Who thought that?" Mica demanded.

Shrugging, Enna and Nissa scanned the sea of grass around them.

"Help me. Someone!"

Mica jumped to his feet and began scouring the nearby area.

"It's not coming from here," Enna sensed. "It's coming from inside the cliffs."

"Is it Gael?"

"No, I don't think it's Gael."

The elves were thoroughly confused. Who else would be calling for help from within the caves?

Narrowing her eyes, Enna stared off to the far cliffs. When she focused her attention, she had superb sight, like a hawk on a mouse in a field far below. The crystals in the cliffs shone in the sunlight. The long grasses swayed in the slight breeze. A few small birds pecked at the ground. However, nothing seemed out of place.

Then, off in the distance, Enna noticed a faint black fog swirling. She watched it whirl in a spiral. Next, like a snake, the black fog uncoiled. It stretched as if taking a great yawn, and then slowly slithered into the solid cliff. A moment later, it had disappeared entirely.

"The black fog," Enna thought, raising her arm to point. But Nissa and Mica had already moved on, marching toward the black cliffs with renewed determination.

This time, as they approached the far cliffs, the cliffs grew bigger. Large quartz crystals jutted from the black rock, just as they had in the cliffs on the opposite side of the meadow. There was, however, no sign of whoever had called for help and no sign of an entrance into the cliffs.

Enna contacted Grandmother and asked for help in finding the entrance. Grandmother consulted her spirits and replied, "There will be a tree next to the cliff. The entrance is close by."

Enna passed on the information to Nissa and Mica. They scoured the cliff for a tree. There were no trees near the cliff. As a matter of fact, there were no trees anywhere.

"What is she talking about, a tree?" Nissa wondered.

"Maybe it's really small," Enna thought. "It's got to be here somewhere."

"Well, let's hurry up and find it. This place is creeping me out more all the time."

Enna nodded. Several yards away a handful of small birds were pecking at the ground. She watched them for a while. They looked harmless enough, minding their own business. *But nothing is as it seems here,* she thought to herself.

They walked east along the cliff, standing on their tiptoes to examine the rock above, crouching down low to spot holes near the ground. They rounded a bend in the cliff and there, standing next to the cliff, was a tree.

It was a good-sized tree, its branches hanging low. Growing on the tree were peaches – dozens of them.

"Peaches!" Enna thought excitedly, plucking one from the branch.

"You're not going to eat that," Nissa thought, eyeing the peach suspiciously.

"Right." Looking sorry, Enna dropped it to the ground.

"So, where's this entrance?" Mica asked, glancing around behind the tree. "Just solid rock back here."

"Maybe up ahead," Enna suggested. They continued their search for an opening into the caves – a hole, a crack, something.

Enna glanced over at the flock of birds. They were still pecking at the ground as before. Somehow, though, they seemed bigger now. One bird sensed that it was being watched and turned to Enna, returning her curious stare.

"What is it?" Nissa asked.

Enna turned back to the cliff. "Nothing, I guess."

"Well, we can't find the entrance," Nissa replied, folding her arms crossly. "Not that I'm surprised, of course."

"This is getting a bit ridiculous," Mica complained, sitting down. "When I signed up for this mission, I thought it would be simple: Enter cave; extract one injured elf; return to village as hero; enjoy afternoon nap." He flicked his tail crankily.

Enna slouched against the rock. *Poor Gael,* she thought to herself miserably. She had tried reaching Gael by thought several times, but there was never any response. She must be unconscious – or worse. A sudden chill swept over Enna as she imagined Gael trapped under a rock in a cold, dark cave, waiting for rescue that wasn't coming.

In addition to being Elffolk's spiritual adviser, Gael was also leader of the village's high council. The high council was made up of retired elves – elves ninety years and older. The council was the highest authority in Elffolk, and council members made decisions for all the villagers. Even Geter, the village chief, reported to them.

"I'll back up and see if I can see the entrance from further away," Nissa suggested tiredly.

Enna just shrugged. She was exhausted, frustrated and feeling more than a little defeated. The entire village had placed Gael's fate in their hands (and paws). What if they failed her?

"Cut that out!" The thoughts were sharp, startling Enna.

"Grandmother?" Enna questioned uncertainly.

"Of course, it's me. Enough with those gloomy thoughts. What's going on there?"

Enna explained their latest mess.

"Hang in there. You're very close. I sense it."

Enna held on to her grandmother's last thoughts. They were close. They had come so far already, and they had only a little further to go. A number of roadblocks had presented themselves, and they'd overcome each one – however narrowly. Surely, they could overcome this last hurdle and rescue Gael.

Of course, Enna didn't know that they still had many more hurdles to go.

Nissa was standing twenty-five yards from the cliff. Using a hand to shield her eyes from the sun, she eyed the cliff carefully.

Enna glanced back to the spot on the ground where the birds had been. They were gone. Funny – she hadn't seen or heard them leave.

"I think I see the entrance," Nissa thought, waving at Enna and Mica.

"Where is it?" Enna wondered, getting to her feet.

"Right beside you! Can't you see it?"

Enna was baffled. She felt along the cliff, inspecting it carefully, but there was no entrance.

"It's right there! It's right there!" Nissa thought, pointing. Then she dropped her arm to her side and wondered why Enna was staring at her in horror.

In that instant, a giant bird swooped out of the sky and plucked Nissa from the earth. Nissa rose into the sky. The bird's thick talons pierced the back of Nissa's shirt, and she hung in the air, stunned one moment, kicking and screaming the next.

Enna and Mica raced to the spot where Nissa had just stood. They stared up into the sky, watching helplessly as the bird carried Nissa higher and higher. At last, the bird turned, gliding toward the black cliffs. It landed somewhere above, disappearing from view.

— CHAPTER SEVEN —

# *In Pursuit of Nissa*

Enna tried to reach her sister by thought, but there was no response.

"What do we do?" Enna asked Mica desperately. Her legs felt weak and wobbly. At any moment, she thought they might collapse under her. She lifted her hands to her face in disbelief. Looking up, she scanned the top of the cliff for any sign of her sister.

The bird and Nissa were nowhere in sight.

"What do we do?" she asked again.

"We go after her," Mica replied. Nodding weakly, she followed him to the cliff. "We climb straight up," he instructed. "I'll go first. There are lots of crystals to hang on to, so this should be easy."

Enna nodded again. She wasn't thinking clearly, and hot tears were blurring her vision. What if they couldn't save Nissa? Suddenly, she felt very sorry for all the mean things she'd ever thought or done to her sister. None of the little things that had annoyed her mattered if Nissa was gone.

"This is no time for crying," Mica reprimanded.

Enna wiped her eyes and sniffed loudly. "OK," she thought. "I can do this."

Mica leaped from one crystal to the next. Enna followed more carefully, wrapping her arms around overhanging crystals and cautiously stepping on to jagged rocks. Her heart was pounding, her hands were shaky, but all she could think was *must save Nissa.*

"It gets harder up here," Mica thought. He was already fifteen feet above Enna. Enna could see that the crystals were thinning out. She made it to the ledge where Mica was resting and inspected the vertical wall above.

"There's a ledge about two yards from here," Enna thought. "But I'll never make it."

Mica eyed the spot carefully, gauging the distance between himself and the ledge, back and forth, back and forth.

Enna looked Mica in the face. "You could do it, Mica."

"I don't know," he thought uncertainly, glancing to the ground far below. "It's a long way to fall."

"You can do it, Mica. Just climb like a mountain goat."

Mica tilted his head to one side and looked at Enna strangely.

"Just like a mountain goat," she encouraged.

"Just like a mountain goat," he thought to himself, summoning all his strength and courage.

"Keep your eyes up."

Pushing off with his hind legs, Mica soared through the air. Enna held her breath. If he didn't reach the ledge, it would be the end of him – that was certain. Even a cat could only fall so far and land on his feet.

Mica reached the ledge and landed expertly. He peered down at Enna, a satisfied look on his face. "Not bad, if I do say so myself," he thought.

Enna clapped. "Keep going!"

She watched with growing confidence as Mica jumped from ledge to ledge, scaling the cliff quickly.

He reached the top of the cliff and looked around. Nissa was lying on a narrow ledge, her body perfectly still.

A piercing cry overhead broke the stillness of the moment. The bird that had seized Nissa was coming in for a landing. It touched down on the ledge, its menacing black talons scraping the rock just inches from Nissa's feet. Flapping its enormous wings, it squawked at Mica fiercely.

Mica arched his back and growled. The bird squawked again, its wings propelling it forward on the ledge.

Mica inched forward, hissing now, baring his teeth. Mica looked fearsome, there was no doubt about it. Still, the bird would not be discouraged. Its black eyes were fixed on Mica, and it held its ground.

Nissa squirmed on the rock ledge just then. Propping herself up with her elbows, she watched the bird, a look of sheer terror frozen on her face.

All at once, Mica raced toward the bird, swiping at it with a paw. He growled, a low feral snarl. A second later, he came in for a second attack, his paw swinging repeatedly.

The bird backed away. Mica stalked forward, quickly closing the distance.

The bird turned, pushing off the ledge. It dipped and soared over the meadow.

Mica turned to Nissa. She was staring at him in disbelief. She rose to her hands and knees and crawled along the ledge.

"How are we going to get down?" she asked.

"I hadn't thought that far ahead," he admitted.

"Are you all right?" Enna asked from below.

"I'm OK," Nissa replied uncertainly, glancing over the ledge. "How do we get down from here?"

There was a long pause, and then Enna replied, "The rope!"

"Do you think you can toss it high enough?"

Enna was wondering the same thing. She had collected the rope into her pack after Mica had rescued them from the quicksand. She climbed back down to the ground and pulled the muddy rope from her pack. Sliding the coiled rope over her shoulder, she proceeded to climb. She would climb as high as she could, and toss the rope from there.

"Is it long enough? Are you sure you can throw it?" Nissa asked again.

*I will,* Enna thought to herself. *I will throw it high enough. It is long enough.* Facing the cliff, she glanced up. Mustering all of her strength, she tossed the rope up, straight up.

"Catch!"

The rope landed at the edge of the ledge where Nissa and Mica were seated. Instinctively, Mica pounced, driving his sharp claws into the rope.

Nissa took the rope from Mica. Anchoring it over a sharp crystal, which jutted from the cliff face, she tied the end around her waist, knotting it twice.

"Come on, Mica," Nissa thought. "You'll have to hold on to me."

Mica examined Nissa uncertainly. He circled her a few times, wondering how best to climb up. Finally, tired of his indecision, Nissa just hoisted him over her shoulder.

"Great spirits, you're heavy," she complained, her knees buckling under the cat's weight.

"It's mostly muscle," Mica replied, a tad defensively. "Muscle weighs more than fat, you know."

"Sure, Mica, sure."

Back on the ground, Enna had tied the other end of the rope around her waist. She then anchored it around a low crystal. This way she could better control the release of the rope, and hopefully, Nissa and Mica wouldn't come down the cliff at warp speed.

"Ready?" Nissa asked, scanning the sky for any sign of the bird.

"Just a minute."

"Come on, Enna!" Nissa thought, swaying unsteadily under Mica's weight. "What are you doing down there, anyway?"

"Don't worry!" Enna was knotting the rope around her waist, making sure it wouldn't come undone. "OK, come on down – slowly."

"Have you anchored the rope?" Nissa questioned.

"Yes."

"Did you tie the rope around your own waist?"

"Yes."

"Now, be sure to release just a bit of slack at a time."

"Will you just trust me and come down?" Enna thought impatiently.

With hands grasping the rope, Nissa cautiously

rappelled from the ledge. Her feet scraped along the cliff, as Enna slowly released the rope upwards.

It was a bumpy, uncomfortable ride, to say the least. More than once, Enna released too much rope, and Nissa and Mica went into free fall, only to come to a jerky, jarring stop. On top of that, Mica's claws were digging into Nissa's back.

"Enna!" Nissa scolded, swinging out from the cliff face and smashing into the rock.

"I'm doing my best!"

Even though Nissa was only halfway down the cliff, Enna could see her rolling her eyes. "Well, your best could be better," Nissa remarked.

*You try it,* Enna thought to herself angrily.

Eventually, Enna seemed to get the hang of the rope. But with just three feet to go, Nissa and Mica dropped again and landed on the ground in a heap.

"Sorry about that," Enna thought, standing over them. "Are you all right?"

"I'll live," Nissa replied.

"Did you get scratched?" Enna asked her sister, thinking of the bird's sharp talons.

"Just by Mica."

"Well, I'm sorry, but my claws are my only means of hanging on," Mica replied touchily.

Enna and Nissa untied the ropes from around their waists. Enna pulled on the rope, and it tumbled to the ground.

"I would say we should be more careful," Enna thought. "But trouble seems to find us here."

— CHAPTER EIGHT —

# *Trouble of Mammoth Proportions*

Enna glanced across the meadow, half expecting the next disaster.

Mica was circling the rope on the ground, examining it from all angles.

"What is it, Mica?"

"I could have sworn this rope was half the length when I found it."

Nissa inspected the rope herself, and then turned to Enna. "Is this the same rope?"

"How many ropes do you think there are lying around in this meadow? Of course it's the same rope."

"Well, it's way longer."

Enna just shook her head. She was weary of the cliffs' games.

Shrugging, Nissa shoved the rope back into the pack.

The afternoon sun slipped behind the cliff, casting a cool shadow over a portion of the meadow. Soon, the entire meadow would be dark and night-time would follow. The thought of spending the night in the crystal caves sent shivers up Enna's spine.

The crystal caves were full of mystery. Things appeared out of nowhere; other things changed and shifted without reason. Enna had dismissed it all as part of the dark magic. Now, there was another explanation lingering at the back of her mind.

Mica was sniffing the air. Nissa walked to his side and stared across the meadow.

Enna frowned. What were they doing? She felt a tingling sensation at the back of her neck. A new threat was looming. She sensed it.

With their backs to the cliff, Enna, Nissa and Mica peered into the tall grasses around them. Anywhere, a predator could be lurking, stalking them, ready to pounce at any time. The creature with the glowing green eyes could be following them still. The black fog could form once again. Or, perhaps the ground would simply open up and swallow them whole in one gigantic gulp. In this place, anything was possible.

Then the ground started shaking.

"Another earthquake!" Enna warned, holding out her arms to steady herself.

"No, it's something else," Nissa thought.

Across the meadow, something was stirring. Enna squinted and tried to make it out. At last, it became clear – an enormous animal was barrelling toward them, the ground thundering under its heavy feet.

"Climb!" Mica directed. He leaped on to a crystal about three feet up the side of the cliff.

The elves didn't follow. Instead, they watched in stunned disbelief as the animal grew closer. They could see it now. It was – well, actually, they had no clue what it was. But huge didn't even begin to describe it. It was the biggest creature they'd ever seen, with enormous white tusks, a long trunk and coarse dark hair covering its body. Most notably, it was charging directly for them.

The animal lowered its head in attack. The sharp ends of its curled tusks lined up with Enna and Nissa.

"What are you waiting for?" Mica demanded. "If you have any desire to live, climb!"

It was no use. Enna and Nissa were so paralyzed with fear, it was as though their feet were glued to the ground.

"I know what this place is," Enna thought suddenly. "I know what's going on."

Nissa glanced at her quickly, and then back at the charging beast.

"We have to imagine that it's not there," Enna added.

Nissa looked at Enna like she'd lost her mind. "What? How?"

"We have to pretend the animal is not there! Just do it!"

Enna squeezed her eyes shut and tried very hard to imagine that a horrible, hairy beast wasn't about to trample her to death in three seconds flat. She opened one eye. The animal was still coming.

"Move!"

Both Enna and Nissa dove to their right, just as the animal tore past them. The animal skidded to an awkward halt to avoid crashing into the cliffs. It turned in a wide circle, preparing to come at them again.

"Why didn't it work?" Nissa demanded.

"I don't know," Enna replied, completely confused. She was certain she had figured out the mystery of the crystal caves. "Maybe we have to actually believe it's not there." She turned to Mica, who was now crouched on a ledge about twenty feet up the side of the cliff. "You, too."

They squeezed their eyes shut again. *OK*, Enna thought to herself. *There is no massive monster charging toward us. It's just me, Nissa and Mica standing in an empty meadow on a beautiful summer day.*

The thundering footsteps stopped. Enna opened her eyes and glanced around. The animal was gone. The meadow was still.

"How can that be?" Nissa asked, her mouth open in amazement.

"You know how Grandmother always tells us that even one little crystal will magnify our thoughts, our energy?" Enna asked. Nissa just nodded. "Well, look around."

They glanced at the cliffs. Everywhere they turned, thousands upon thousands of crystals surrounded them.

"So, whatever we think comes true?" Nissa asked.

"Yes," Enna replied.

"All right, so who's responsible for thinking that a huge, hairy beast would come to kill us?" Mica demanded.

Nissa shook her head. Enna frowned, second guessing her theory. "Well, maybe it's not just what we imagine. Maybe it's what we feel, too."

"OK, so who had a *feeling* that a huge, hairy beast would come to kill us?" Mica demanded again.

"That's not what I mean," Enna thought. "I mean, our fear has been growing since we arrived at these crystal caves. As a result, our fear has been creating scary things."

Nissa and Mica paused to consider her theory.

"Our hopes have created things, too," Nissa added after some further thought, "like the rope. When Mica needed something to pull us out of the quicksand, a rope appeared. When you needed the rope to be longer in order to rescue me, it was longer."

"When we tried crossing the meadow the first time, we were feeling down, and the black cliffs seemed to get further away," Mica added. "After we rested and ate, we walked to the cliffs without a problem."

The elves nodded.

"That's why I say never underestimate the power of food and rest," Mica added wisely.

Enna reflected on the events that had occurred and the creatures they'd encountered in the short time they'd been in the crystal caves. There was the cave dweller, the quicksand, the bird, the charging beast, the black fog, even Mica's juicy, monster-sized rodents. Had they created all of it? Was any of it real?

"We'll have to be more careful with our thoughts," Nissa realized.

"We have to believe that we'll rescue Gael and find a safe way back out," Enna added.

"Rescue Gael. Get the heck out," Mica repeated. "Sounds like a good plan to me."

— CHAPTER NINE —

# *King of the Crystal Caves*

They turned back to the cliff and stared at the peach tree for several minutes.

"Grandmother told me to call upon the spirits if we needed help," Enna thought.

"OK, so do it," Nissa nodded.

"Who should I call upon?"

"How should I know? Whoever is available, I guess."

Enna pursed her lips together and closed her eyes. She'd never summoned the spirits before. "Good spirits," she concentrated. "If you're not too busy, would you mind helping us find the entrance to the caves?"

She opened her eyes and stared at the peach tree. Out of nothing, a wispy spirit appeared.

"I'm Kaya," the spirit thought. Draped in a long white dress, with long black hair cascading over her shoulders, Kaya was the most beautiful creature they'd ever seen. A warm smile broke over Kaya's face.

"Can you help us?" Enna asked.

"This way," Kaya replied. She turned to the cliff and walked straight through the solid rock, disappearing as quickly as she'd appeared.

"Well, that's not very helpful at all," Mica thought irritably, sitting back down. "I mean, that's fine if you can walk through walls, but some of us are three-dimensional, you know? Some spirits...." He turned his face away in disgust and flicked his tail hard against the ground.

Enna and Nissa walked to the spot where Kaya had vanished. The rock face appeared completely solid. However, when Enna reached to touch the cliff, she found that her hand slipped through.

"It's here, Mica!" Enna thought excitedly. "You can't see it, but it's here!" She turned to Nissa, who was staring at the cliff suspiciously, slowly poking at the rock with one finger, watching the finger disappear, and then pulling it back quickly.

"I guess I'll go first," Enna thought with a twinge of annoyance.

"It should be fine," Nissa nodded, but her skeptical expression did not instill confidence.

With arms extended before her, Enna walked into the cliff. She watched as her fingers, hands and wrists disappeared before her very eyes. With a mixture of unease and excitement, she pressed on. For three whole steps, everything went black – pitch black. She stood completely still, waiting impatiently for her eyes to adjust to the darkness.

Gradually, her surroundings became visible. She was standing inside a tall chamber. The cave continued to her right and to her left. Somewhere she heard the faint sound of water falling over rocks.

Enna turned back to the rock wall that she'd just

passed through. It was now perfectly solid. Where were Nissa and Mica?

Lighting her lantern, Enna glanced around some more. Then she waited. A minute passed, then another and another. She closed her eyes and imagined Nissa standing next to her. A few seconds later, Nissa appeared. Enna clutched Nissa's hands excitedly, and Nissa screamed.

"It's just me," Enna thought. "Your eyes will adjust in a minute."

They waited for Mica, willing him to appear. However, no amount of willing could bring it to be. They tried communicating with him by thought, but there was no reply. They paced the chamber impatiently, glancing over at the cave wall every few seconds to see whether he'd arrived.

About ten minutes later, Mica finally appeared. He glanced around, with ears perked up and nose sniffing, his yellow eyes glowing in the dark. Then he lowered his face and licked his chops.

"Mica, what took you so long?" Enna asked. "We were so worried!"

"No need to worry. I can take care of myself," Mica thought. "Unlike a couple of elves who need constant rescuing."

"Were you eating again?" Enna demanded. "Is that what took you so long?"

"Eating again?" Mica repeated, offended. "May I remind you that it had been hours since I last ate? Besides, I have low blood sugar."

"You do not!" Enna argued.

Mica just turned his head, clearly insulted.

The cave was cool and damp. Yet, impossibly, the faint scent of flowers lingered in the air.

"Which way?" Nissa wondered.

"This way," came the thought. Kaya appeared again. Effortlessly, she floated over the ground, her white dress trailing behind her. As they followed, they realized the floral scent was coming from her.

"How far do you think it is?" Enna asked Nissa.

Nissa just shrugged in response.

"Not far," Kaya replied. Enna glanced at Nissa in surprise. Kaya had accessed her thoughts. She hadn't meant for Kaya to hear her thoughts at all. *The spirits are powerful,* Enna realized.

They slipped through the cave. Kaya moved quickly, and Enna and Nissa found themselves running just to keep up.

The sound of falling water grew loud as they entered a large cavern. On the far side of the cavern, water poured from the ceiling, collecting in a pool on the floor, and draining away somewhere below. Across the ground, fragments of rocks and crystals were scattered.

"Where is Gael?" Enna asked, turning to Kaya – but Kaya was gone.

"Gael was here," came a reply.

An old elf in a long white cape swept into the cavern. "This is where she lay," the elf declared, pounding his wooden cane on the ground theatrically. Then he glanced around and brought a hand to his chin. He turned around suddenly, his white cape swinging behind him.

"Or over here," he thought, motioning to a pile of broken rocks. He seemed less sure of himself this time.

"It could have been here," he added with a sigh, stepping forward several feet.

"It doesn't matter," Nissa interrupted. "Where is she now?"

The strange old elf glanced up quickly, as if he had momentarily forgotten their presence. His expression changed from frustration to pure joy.

"Pleasure to meet you," he thought, beaming. He extended both arms in the traditional elf embrace. Tentatively, Nissa stepped forward, holding out her arms. He clasped her hands in his. "Meltick's the name, or King Mel, if you prefer. King of the crystal caves, that is."

"If he's king of the caves, then I'm king of the cats," Mica thought, settling on to his side, eyeing the elf curiously.

Enna shot him a glare. "Don't be so rude!"

King Mel moved toward Enna. His hair was long and white, and his beard hung to his belly. For an elf, he was uncommonly tall.

As he entered the lantern's light, his face became visible. With milky eyes, sagging cheeks and a long drooping nose, his features were most unpleasant. In fact, "unattractive" would be too generous.

"You're probably wondering why I'm so tall," the old elf surmised, smiling at Enna.

"Yes," Enna replied politely. "That is what I was thinking."

"I wished it so," he winked. "Here in these crystal caves, anything is possible."

Enna nodded, but privately she wondered why he hadn't wished for good looks.

"Do you know where Gael is?" Nissa asked.

"No," King Mel replied, pounding his cane on the ground for effect. Then his eyes narrowed. "But I have my suspicions." He glanced around the cavern, as if the answers may be written on the walls. "A whole lot of suspicions," he added, half to himself.

"Would you mind sharing them?" Nissa asked, frowning impatiently. "That's why we're here. We've come to rescue Gael."

"Ah, I see. Well, I didn't think you'd come for a holiday." He chuckled at his own joke. Then, very quickly, his expression turned solemn as a new thought crossed his mind. "We don't get many visitors," he added heavily.

Then King Mel turned on his heel, flourishing his cane in a motion that was likely meant to beckon. "Come, I'll show you to my living quarters."

Nissa turned to Enna and held up her arms in question. "What about Gael?"

Enna just shrugged. "I say we go with him. Come on, Mica."

"If it's all the same to you, I think I'll just catch a few Z's," Mica replied. "Been a long day, lots of exertion, very little relaxation." He circled on the spot a few times, and finally settled on to the stone floor. "Tell me everything that happens, though. It's not every day you get to spend time with a king."

Enna ignored his sarcasm.

King Mel was waiting for them in a tunnel off the

cavern. "This way," he pointed down the dark tunnel. Then he broke into a run as if he was chasing someone. As he ran, his white cape floated up behind him.

"Why is he running?" Nissa asked Enna, as they sprinted to keep up.

"I have no idea."

A moment later, they had exited the caves and were standing at the edge of the grassy meadow. Enna glanced back at the large opening to the caves. Why hadn't they seen it before?

She turned to King Mel in bewilderment. "It was that easy to get into the caves?"

"Sure," King Mel replied. "What? Did you expect it to be hard?"

"Well, yeah!"

"I see. Well, that's why it was hard for you. I just head straight for the cave wall, fully expecting to find an exit, and there it is. I find it helps if you run – tricks your mind into believing there must be an opening if you're running flat out toward it." He glanced around curiously, eyeing the meadow with great interest.

"Our expectations come true in this place, don't they?" Enna asked, interrupting King Mel's personal thoughts.

"Yes, as they do everywhere," he replied distractedly. "But here, with the crystals multiplying our energy so many times, our thoughts and expectations come about much faster."

"Our thoughts and beliefs become our reality in regular life, too," Enna added, remembering the teachings. "Usually it takes longer for things to come into being. There's more time to have conflicting thoughts and feelings that cancel out the earlier ones. So if you want something, you need to think clearly and really focus on what you want – and stay focused. Also, when you get inspired, you need to take action – take steps toward your goal." Enna smiled to herself. Grandmother would be proud. She had recalled the teaching perfectly.

King Mel hadn't been following Enna's thoughts. He looked startled when he caught her gaze and she was waiting for him to respond.

"Right, sure," he thought quickly, trying to disguise the fact that he hadn't been paying attention. He gazed at the surrounding black cliffs with a look of adoration. "Here, our thoughts become our reality before our very eyes. It's a wondrous, magical place, these crystal caves. But it's a dangerous place, too. You have to pay attention to your thoughts, feelings and beliefs at all times."

"Yeah, so we discovered," Enna replied.

King Mel led the elves across the meadow. "I see you created a meadow."

"We created this?"

"Yep," King Mel replied. "This was just a small clearing last time I came through."

Through an archway in the western cliffs, the elves stepped into an enormous cavern. Long crystals dripped from the ceiling. A solid sheet of white quartz lined the floor. In every corner, crystal vases overflowed with flowers. And in the very centre of the room, a large crystal throne rested on a thick slab of black rock.

Spinning in circles, Enna and Nissa stared in awe at the crystal palace.

"It's amazing, isn't it?" King Mel beamed, his chest swelling with pride.

The elves nodded, breathing in the scent of the flowers. "How long have you lived here?" Enna wondered.

The proud smile remained on his face as he replied, "A long time."

"Why haven't we heard of you?" Nissa asked.

"I keep to myself. No need to leave the crystal caves." He looked around the room as if he, too, was seeing it with fresh eyes. "It was when the elves were first settling the village of Elffolk that I discovered these caves. And, well, I just never left."

"But that was over 200 years ago," Enna interrupted.

"Sounds about right."

Enna and Nissa eyed him carefully. Could he really be so old? They'd never known an elf to live past 140 years.

"So, you live here alone?" Enna asked.

"No, there are a few others."

"Do any of them have glowing green eyes and make scratching sounds?" Nissa asked dryly.

They watched as King Mel's eyes narrowed and his expression turned sour. "Ah, then you've run into one of the Egoz."

"Do you think the Egoz took Gael?" Enna asked.

King Mel sighed deeply and nodded.

Enna and Nissa glanced at each other uncertainly. "Are the Egoz friends of yours?"

"Not so much friends, no." He shook his head. Then he grunted, as if he was growing more repulsed by the idea by the second. "No, definitely not."

"What would they want with Gael?" Nissa asked impatiently.

"I don't know," King Mel replied mysteriously.

"Well, what are they doing in the crystal caves?" Nissa asked.

King Mel stepped up to his crystal throne, held out his arms as if someone was taking his cape from him, and seated himself.

"For centuries the crystal caves have drawn all sorts of creatures – elves and big folk," he began. "Wish fulfilment can be a blessing, but it can also be a curse. It's not always in your best interest to get what you think you want. Yet, the idea of wish fulfilment continues to attract, always holding the promise of something better, something more. Alas, there are few who can resist its temptation." He held up an arm dramatically and stared off into nothing as if he had just delivered a great speech.

"Is that why you came?" Enna asked.

"I like to think not," King Mel replied. "You see, it takes great discipline of the mind to live here where one's thoughts, emotions and beliefs come into being almost instantly. To be truly joyful, one must be pure of thought, clear of inner baggage. That is true everywhere, of course. But here, we are constantly reminded of this truth because our thoughts come about so quickly. So, it is the perfect place to test one's clarity of mind. That's why I chose to stay."

He smiled down at Enna and Nissa from his massive throne.

"You said the Egoz are here for a different reason."

"Right," King Mel nodded. "The Egoz were lured into the crystal caves by the promise of material things, of eternal youth and beauty, and of ease and fortune."

"Did they find those things?" Enna asked.

"Sure, they found them, at first. However, without inner peace and joy, those things are hollow. After a time, they felt the emptiness. Still, they wanted more."

He slammed a fist on to the armrest of his throne to emphasize his point. Then he winced, shaking his hand.

"They tried to mask their feelings of lack with more," he continued. "They became addicted to the idea of more, constantly searching for the one thing that would bring them true joy."

"They never found it, did they?" Enna thought.

"True happiness can never be found outside of ourselves," King Mel replied. "If some *thing* makes you happy, you're dependent on having that thing. As soon as that thing is gone, your happiness is gone.

"This place is said to be cursed by a dark magic. Yet, there is nothing dark or evil about the crystals. These crystals are, by nature, neutral. They simply multiply energy – positive or negative. It makes no difference to them."

"So, did the crystals magnify the Egoz' feelings of lack and emptiness?"

"Indeed, they're a miserable old bunch." King Mel shook his head sadly. "The beautiful things they created have crumbled and rotted. The fortunes they built have been lost. Their own beauty has faded horribly. But still they stay on in these crystal caves, clinging to the only truth they know – a false truth – that they will find what they're looking for somewhere out there."

"Have you tried to help them?" Enna asked.

King Mel pursed his lips together into a tight line and cast his eyes downward. "I've not been able to help them. The Egoz grew so consumed by the material world, they lost their ability to communicate by thought. They created their own primitive language – grunts and howls. It's frightening to hear them in the blackest hours of the night." A haunted look overtook him.

"Are they dangerous?" Nissa asked.

"We have an agreement to stay out of each other's way. I keep to the western cliffs and caves. The Egoz stay in the eastern caves. I've never breached the agreement, and no harm has ever come to me. However, they're not very friendly toward visitors, I'm afraid. Now that they know you're here, I'm not sure what they'll do."

"Are the Egoz elves?" Nissa wondered.

"Elves," King Mel repeated, and looked as though he was recalling a very faraway memory. "I'm not sure what you'd call them now, but, yes, they were once elves."

— CHAPTER TEN —

# *The Egoz*

Across the meadow, the eastern cliffs loomed. Enna and Nissa knew what they had to do. If there was a chance that Gael had been captured by the Egoz, they had to go into the eastern caves after her.

Enna found Mica asleep in the cave exactly where she'd left him.

"Get up!" she thought, standing over him. He opened a single eye, looked at Enna with disinterest and promptly fell back asleep.

"We're leaving, Mica."

"Just another five minutes," Mica thought tiredly.

"We have to go, now!"

"Three minutes."

"Suit yourself. Hopefully, the Egoz don't find you."

Slowly, Mica raised his head. "OK, who are the Egoz?"

"Oh, just that creepy cave dweller with glowing green eyes that followed us through the caves. Except there's a whole bunch of them. King Mel thinks they took Gael."

"All right, all right. I'm going." Reluctantly, and in a very foul mood, Mica followed Enna to the meadow where Nissa and King Mel were waiting.

An anxious feeling was growing inside Enna as she glanced up at the eastern cliffs. Somewhere within those dark caves, the Egoz lurked. Perhaps they were watching her now.

She contacted Grandmother and described King Mel and the Egoz. Grandmother sensed Enna's fear and reminded her to focus on her goal – finding Gael. Gradually, Enna's worries faded into the background.

Solemnly, they crept across the meadow. Behind them, the sky was aglow in shades of pink and purple. Most evenings, a sunset like that was a sight to behold. However, on this occasion, the setting sun marked the end of the day and the coming darkness. And no one wanted to spend the night in the crystal caves.

"We'll need to move quickly," King Mel directed. "The Egoz are most active at night."

"No time for a snack, in that case?" Mica wondered. Enna just shot him a weary look. "Just checking," he added. "Didn't think so. But it never hurts to ask."

"I don't even know how you can think about food at a time like this," Enna thought.

"A time like this?"

"We're entering the Egoz' territory, Mica. The Egoz live in the eastern caves, and that's where we're going."

"Ah well, see, I didn't know that," Mica replied. After some careful thought, he added, "Though, that knowledge didn't affect my appetite at all."

Enna laughed as Mica strode along beside her. Even in the darkest hour, he somehow managed to lighten the mood.

As they walked on, a question popped into Enna's mind. "King Mel, do you know why Gael contacted Eiffel? I mean, of all the elves she could have contacted, why him?"

"It wasn't Gael who contacted Eiffel," King Mel answered. "Kaya told me what happened, and I alerted Eiffel."

"*You* alerted Eiffel? But why him?"

"Eiffel and I go way back. We knew each other from the early days of Elffolk."

"So, Eiffel's that old, too," Enna realized, and glanced up at King Mel. "Sorry, I didn't mean to suggest that you're old."

"No need to apologize," King Mel replied, waving his hand dismissively. "I am, as you say, old. No two ways about it." He stared at the ground with a frown and a ponderous look, as if he was only now just realizing how very old he was.

They arrived at the eastern cliffs and stared at the black rock wall before them. King Mel pulled the group into a huddle and explained the way through the eastern caves. With the end of his cane, he drew a crude map in the dirt.

The elves studied the map, memorizing every twist and turn.

"This is where I believe you'll find Gael," King Mel added, pounding the end of his cane into the centre of his drawing and destroying the entire map in the process. Then his expression turned dour. "There's one more thing I should mention."

"Is it about the black fog?" Enna asked quickly. She

had been itching to ask about it. Turning it over in her mind, she wondered whether she had created it, along with the other frightening creatures they'd encountered.

"The black fog," King Mel thought, narrowing his eyes. "Also known as Belial."

"Belial?" Nissa and Enna repeated.

"That's his name."

"So the black fog is real?" Enna asked. "It's not just something I created?"

"Oh, it was created," King Mel replied. "But not here, and not by any of us." For the first time since Enna and Nissa had met King Mel, he appeared genuinely fearful. But the expression on his face quickly faded, as he gained control over his emotions.

Nissa and Enna waited for King Mel to explain, but as usual, he needed some prompting.

"Who created Belial, and what's he doing here?"

"Belial was created by the big people, but for what purpose, I haven't the faintest idea. He has only just come to the crystal caves, likely drawn to the unhappy energy of the Egoz."

"Like attracts like," Enna thought, remembering her teachings.

"He is a powerful force," King Mel continued. "My intuition tells me he is growing stronger all the time."

The fine hairs on Enna's arms rose as she recalled her encounter with Belial. There was indeed something very sinister about him.

"We should get going," Nissa thought. "It will be night soon."

King Mel led the group to an opening in the eastern cliffs. Enna and Nissa thanked him for his trouble. Then, with a royal wave, the king of the crystal caves watched his guests depart into the blackness.

An uneasy feeling overcame Enna the moment she stepped inside the caves. The temperature dropped, the light grew dim and the air smelled horribly dank and foul.

With a sleeve over her nose to block the stench, she pressed on, deeper into the home of the Egoz. They were trespassers now – trespassers in forbidden territory. Who knew what the Egoz would do if they found them.

They crept through a winding tunnel, the lantern lighting the path just ahead. Enna ran her hand along the rock wall and found it cold and slimy. Pulling her hand away in disgust, she examined it under the lantern light. Her hand was wet – nothing more. She held up the lantern and spotted a tiny stream of water trickling down the wall.

They arrived at a fork in the tunnel. According to King Mel, they were to turn left. The passage to the left was perfectly round, as if a gigantic earthworm had passed through, carving out the tunnel.

Enna, Nissa and Mica were stealthy travellers when they needed to be – quick and light of foot. The elves' feet were small and their shoes soft, so they made little sound as they walked. However, when it came to stealth, Mica had them all beat. He led the way in near perfect silence.

"Does it seem like the tunnel is getting smaller?" Nissa wondered.

Stretching out her arms, Enna could touch both sides

of the tunnel. When they had first entered the round tunnel, it was nearly twice as wide. "I thought it was all in my head," Enna thought, sucking in a sharp breath. "You know, my fear of small spaces."

Like a giant funnel, the tunnel became smaller and smaller until the elves had to keep their heads ducked and their arms tucked at their sides.

"Um, do you see an opening up ahead?" Enna asked Mica, trying to control her anxiety.

"Nothing yet."

Enna exhaled a long, slow breath. She would only go so far, she told herself. If it got to a point where she had to squeeze through something tight, she would stop and turn around. She refused to push her way through any more narrow tunnels or cracks.

"There's a dim light up ahead," Mica thought. "It looks like a perfectly round hole."

"A hole?" Enna repeated. "How big is it?"

"Can't tell yet, but we're almost there."

*Good thing,* Enna thought to herself, now crawling on her hands and knees. Her head was brushing the ceiling and her shoulders were scraping the sides of the tunnel. They *had* to be almost there, or very soon they'd be slithering through the tunnel like snakes.

Enna arrived at the hole and her heart sank. The hole was very small. She had promised herself she wouldn't squeeze through another small space, yet the idea of crawling backwards through the tunnel did not appeal to her, either.

Enna passed the pack and lantern to Nissa behind her.

Her heart was beating madly in her chest. She hated small spaces, she just hated them. *Just get it over with*, Enna thought to herself. On the count of ten she pushed her way through the hole and slid to the floor. A second later, she felt a heavy weight on her chest.

"Ouch, Nissa! You just stepped on me."

"Well, why are you lying on the floor?"

"I need a minute," Enna explained, her heart still racing.

"I could use a minute, too," Mica agreed, sitting next to her. "You know what else I could use?"

"A cat treat?" Enna asked tiredly.

"You bet."

Enna untied the bundle at Mica's side, retrieving a handful of cat treats. "You're running low, Mica."

Mica was too busy enjoying the moment to worry about his future supply.

Enna glanced around for the first time. They were in a spacious cavern, surrounded by huge crystal columns.

"These are the biggest crystals I've ever seen," Nissa remarked, staring at the massive structures all around her.

While Nissa admired the crystals and Mica licked his paws, Enna wandered around in the cavern. Each crystal column had six smooth sides. Some were a murky white, others perfectly clear. A faint light on the far side of the cavern drew Enna across the room. There she discovered a doorway.

She peered through the doorway, which led to another chamber. The room was dark, though Enna sensed it was very large as well. In the opposite corner of the room, a soft light appeared. Quietly, Enna crept forward. The light in the far corner moved. More than that, it was speaking.

"In those early days, huge animals roamed the island of Atlantis."

Enna held her breath, but she continued to inch forward. The light was mesmerizing. As she approached, she realized the light was in the shape of a person – a very tall person. It moved like a real person, but it was transparent.

"What is it?" Enna wondered.

"A hologram," came the reply. Suddenly, Kaya was standing next to her.

"What's a hologram?" Enna asked.

"It's a three-dimensional image," Kaya replied. "This one comes from a memory stored in the crystals."

"The animals were the fiercest predators one could imagine," the hologram continued. "Huge birds with incredible wingspans swooped out of the sky and carried away full-grown humans. Giant animals speared their prey with gigantic tusks, and then trampled them just to be sure they were dead. Terrifying sea monsters patrolled the ocean shores, swallowing sailors and small boats in one gulp. They were everywhere – these deadly animals – and they nearly destroyed all human life."

The hologram appeared as a kindly old woman. White wavy hair hung about her shoulders, and she wore loose fitting robes. Even in the dimness of the room, her eyes were as blue as the sky on a clear summer day. Her lips were moving and she was making the strangest sounds – *words*. Yet, Enna could understand what she was saying.

She was picking up on the thoughts before the words.

"Does she see me?" Enna wondered.

"She can't see you because she's long dead," Kaya replied. "This memory is thousands of years old."

The hologram continued on about vicious attacks and the failed attempts of humans to defend themselves.

"Finally, a meeting was held, where the humans decided to work together for the first time in ages," the hologram said. "They used their brains to outsmart the deadly animals. Eventually, the humans won. They defeated the animals – all except the sea monsters. The sea monsters moved off the shorelines, but they still roam the oceans."

Moving closer to the hologram, Enna waved a hand before its lifelike face. She turned to Kaya. "The huge, hairy beast that tried to trample us, and the giant bird that stole Nissa – were they memories stored in the crystals?"

"Clever elf. Yes, your fears unleashed memories that were held in the crystals. You conjured up creatures that had been long extinct in Atlantis."

"How many memories are saved in these crystals?" Enna wondered, glancing around at a room full of crystals.

"More than we could possibly count," Kaya replied. "The crystals store all kinds of energy and information."

Enna continued to watch the hologram in amazement. The hologram explained how the humans had survived the animal attacks over the years. Some of the humans had lived in caves or found shelter high in tree tops. Others had built homes on the sides of cliffs. Still others had moved underground. The humans had used their primitive tools to fight off the animals. However, the animals outnumbered the humans, and the tools weren't enough to stop them. It wasn't until the humans came together that they were able to defeat the animals.

Suddenly, a grunting sound filled the cavern, echoing off the walls.

Enna turned, squinting in the dim light. Who – or what – had grunted? She scanned the room, but there was no one in sight. Even Kaya had vanished.

Then, in the shadowy corners of the room, a slender figure shifted. Perched on the edge of a chair, it crossed its twiggy legs. Long white strands of hair hung around its face and fell to the floor. It lifted its head and two green eyes shone in the darkness.

Enna moved closer and held back a gasp. The creature had grey skin, brittle hair and an overall ghostly air.

"Who are you?" Enna asked in thought, but there was no reply. The creature just stared at Enna with a vacant expression. Then the creature's lips parted, strange sounds tumbling out. Enna couldn't understand a single word.

*An Egoz*, Enna realized. She froze in her tracks. What would it do to her?

"We're looking for our friend, Gael," Enna explained in a rush when the Egoz stopped speaking. "We've come to take her home. Please, can you tell us where we can find her?"

The creature wasn't registering any of Enna's thoughts. It just looked at her curiously, cocking its thin grey head to one side.

All at once, Enna remembered what King Mel had said – the Egoz had lost the ability to communicate telepathically.

The eyes of the Egoz were so empty, so cold, Enna had to look away. Slowly, she backed away from the creature. Still perched on its chair, the Egoz simply watched her with the same mild curiosity.

"We have to go," Enna thought to Nissa and Mica as she rushed past them. She plucked the lantern and pack from the ground and tore off into the adjoining tunnel. "The Egoz know we're here!"

## — CHAPTER ELEVEN —

# *Prisoners*

According to King Mel's map, they had only to pass through one final chamber before arriving in the heart of the Egoz' territory. This was where King Mel believed Gael was being held prisoner.

With aching legs and empty stomachs, Enna, Nissa and Mica pressed on. They didn't bother complaining as they were all in the same boat – well, save for Mica whose stomach was never really empty.

Just as King Mel's map had indicated, the tunnel led to another cavern. They stopped in the centre of the dark chamber and glanced around. Their eyes widened. They stared in horror.

From every corner of the cavern, glowing green eyes stared back.

They were surrounded by ten or more Egoz. Enna stole a glance to the tunnel leading off the cavern. An Egoz blocked the exit. She looked to the tunnel they'd just come through. There stood another Egoz, its green eyes staring.

There was no escape.

One Egoz moved out of the shadows and into the light of the lantern.

At the very sight of it, Enna shuddered. In the light, the Egoz' eyes switched from green to black. Its skin was grey, its hair tangled, its clothing tattered. With quivering lips, it bared broken, yellow teeth.

"We mean you no harm," Enna thought quickly. "We've just come for Gael. She's one of our elders and the village's spiritual adviser, and well, we really need her back. I'm sure there's something we could do for you, in return. Is there anything you need from the village? Some new clothes, maybe? A hairbrush?" The Egoz just stared, its expression unchanging.

Suddenly, bony hands seized Enna and Nissa, long, sharp nails digging into their upper arms. A net was tossed over Mica. Before anyone could resist or protest or attempt escape, they were dragged through a tunnel and into complete darkness. The tunnel sloped downward. As they descended the air grew danker and more foul.

They were taken to a room. At last, the bony fingers released their grip on Enna and Nissa, and the elves sank to the ground. With a shake of the net, Mica was hurled into the room after them. Landing on his feet, he turned and hissed at his captor. A heavy stone door slammed shut, locking them in.

The room was so dark, Enna couldn't see her hands in front of her. Still her eyes darted around the room, trying desperately to focus on something.

With the best night vision, Mica offered to inspect the room. He returned a minute later with a full report. "We have comfortable chairs, a low table, a fireplace and a mantel. Maybe we're not prisoners after all. Maybe this is how the Egoz treat their guests."

"This is no time for jokes, Mica," Nissa warned.

"No joke," Mica replied.

Enna and Nissa crawled across the hard floor. Then their hands touched down on the softest surface they'd felt all day – a rug. A few seconds later, Enna bumped her head. Reaching up with one arm, she felt the edge of a chair. She eased her way up into the seat and exhaled slowly.

A light came on.

"What just happened?" Enna asked.

"I found a lamp," Nissa answered. She was lying on a long chair, her legs crossed at the ankle. If you didn't know Nissa was a prisoner of the Egoz, trapped far beneath the earth, you might very well think she was visiting friends.

Mica was sitting on a chair opposite Enna. He wrapped his tail around himself.

They stared at each other. What was this place?

"Maybe all the dungeons are in use," Mica suggested lightly.

"King Mel said that the Egoz had created beautiful things," Enna recalled.

"Yeah, but he said all their beautiful things had rotted and crumbled."

They glanced around. The furniture in the room *was* beautiful, and nothing showed even the first signs of rotting or crumbling.

"What's this?" Nissa wondered, picking up a piece of material from the floor.

Enna leaned toward Nissa for a closer look. The

material was white, oval shaped, with purple embroidery used by the elves.

"It's Gael's handkerchief," Enna realized excitedly. "She must have left it for us, to let us know she was here!"

"Well, if she's here and she's fine, why isn't she returning any of our thoughts?" Nissa wondered.

Enna frowned. It didn't make sense at all.

All at once, a fire ignited in the fireplace in the corner of the room, bursting from nothing. A moment later, it was roaring and crackling in full force.

Then on the table before them, platters of food appeared – grapes, apples and slices of cheese.

Nissa and Enna stared in awe. Mica leaped on to the table, sniffing the food hungrily.

Nissa gasped. "Don't you dare eat it!"

"Why not?" Mica's gaze was fixed on the cheese. He glanced at Nissa who was fiercely shaking her head, and hurriedly gobbled a slice.

Frozen with fear, Enna and Nissa watched Mica, wondering what would happen to him.

He caught their horrified expressions and licked his chops. "Delicious."

"No more!" Nissa warned, leaning forward in her chair. But Mica was already devouring the next piece of cheese.

"Exquisite."

"Stop it, Mica. Stop it!"

Tauntingly, Mica plucked a third piece of cheese from the platter, holding it between his teeth. All the while, he stared at Nissa. Nissa reached out to grab the cheese from him, but he dropped it into his mouth.

"Scrumptious."

Wrapping her arms around Mica's waist, Nissa hauled him off the low table.

"Hey, cut that out," he complained. "You'll give me indigestion."

"I think Mica will be fine," Enna thought, observing the scene from her chair.

"How can you think that?" Nissa asked, watching Mica worriedly.

"Mica believes he'll be fine," Enna thought. "Now if you ate it, it would be another story."

Nissa sighed as Mica stood on his hind legs and licked the tray. "So what do we do now?" she asked.

Enna contacted Grandmother with the details of their latest crisis.

"I'm not getting any more images," Grandmother replied. "Something inside the Egoz' caves is blocking my thoughts. All I can suggest is that you wait."

They followed Grandmother's advice. Even if they could find a way to escape their prison, the Egoz still had Gael. And they couldn't leave without her.

Mica wandered to the fireplace and stretched luxuriously before the roaring fire. "I must say, if you have to be thrown into prison, it could be worse," he thought. In under a minute, he was fast asleep.

"Honestly, that cat doesn't worry about anything," Nissa thought irritably. "How can you even think about sleep at a time like this? Here we are, trapped in a cave, and who knows what the Egoz are going to…." She stopped mid-sentence and gaped at Enna.

Enna's eyelids were growing heavy as she watched the flames flicker in the fireplace. With her head resting against the back of the chair, she was very nearly asleep herself. It was well past her bedtime, and it had been a very full day. At that moment, sleep was the most welcome idea to wash over her. Nissa's thoughts faded into the background.

Enna woke some time later. Mica was still fast asleep, his chest rising and falling deeply with each breath. Nissa had fallen asleep as well. She was lying on her side across the long chair, her hands folded neatly under her head like a pillow. The fire was still crackling in the fireplace, working at logs that never seemed to burn down.

On the stone mantel above the fireplace, a tall crystal vase held a bouquet of purple flowers. *Flowers, in this place?*

Above the mantel there was a painting of a beautiful, but unfamiliar landscape. A city of tall white buildings perched at the edge of a rocky cliff, overlooking a vast turquoise ocean. Beyond the city, a row of snow-capped mountains stretched into the clouds.

Nissa yawned and rubbed her eyes. "Did I fall asleep?"

The door burst open just then, and an Egoz stood in the doorway. He glanced around the room in astonishment, his gaze sweeping the furniture, the fireplace and the walls. Enna followed his gaze. Much to her own amazement, the walls were painted and decorated with pictures. She glanced around the room and saw that there was even more furniture than she'd realized, including a dining table with place settings for eight.

A rare smile flashed across the Egoz' face. He beckoned the elves to come. Cautiously, they rose to their feet.

Without a lantern to guide them, they were directed down a long, dark passageway. The Egoz prodded them from behind with a long walking stick.

Somewhere in the shuffle, Enna fell behind the others. She heard their footsteps fade ahead of her, but in the blackness she couldn't see where they had gone. She felt her way along the tunnel, and came to a door on her right. Pushing open the door she found herself in a cavern.

She couldn't see a thing, but she could tell the cavern was very big. Water dripped from the ceiling, each drop echoing across the room. The air was cool and damp.

She stepped deeper into the cavern, holding out her arms in front of her. Even before her eyes adjusted to the darkness, she sensed she was not alone. Then, when her eyes finally did adjust, she almost wished they hadn't.

A thin black fog was swirling before her. She stumbled back a few steps and slammed into the rough rock wall behind her.

With a queasy feeling in her stomach, Enna watched as the black fog transformed into a solid, humanoid mass. At first, it was just an outline, but it filled in quickly, the details of its face becoming clearer by the second.

Enna opened her mouth to scream, but no sound escaped. The dark figure before her was neither human nor animal. Rather, it was a mixture of both. It had the body of a man, but the eyes and horns of a bull.

"Belial," she thought. The dark figure smiled in reply.

His dark gaze seemed to bore into her, and she felt her legs weakening.

"Trespasser," Belial replied. His thoughts were unlike any telepathic thought she'd ever received. They were like a hiss inside her mind.

"I have no quarrel with the Egoz," Enna explained hurriedly. "I'm only here to rescue Gael. As soon as I have her, I'll be on my way."

"Troublemaker," Belial hissed.

"No trouble," Enna thought, shaking her head. "I mean, I'm not up to any trouble, if that's what you mean. I'm not here to trouble the Egoz. Live and let live, that's what I say. I'm just here to save my friend Gael. Well, she's not so much a friend as our most respected spiritual adviser." She stopped. She was rambling and Belial was smirking.

"Fraud," he accused.

Enna frowned. *Fraud?*

Belial extended a hand, and Enna recoiled in horror. His fingers were unusually long, his fingernails sharp and black. Enna was trying desperately to recall the ancient teachings that Grandmother had explained to her. There was something about good and evil, light and darkness. Something about light overcoming darkness....

*In the light, all darkness dissolves.*

That was it. Enna shut her eyes and imagined a brilliant, bright light surrounding her. She envisioned it growing, filling up the cavern from floor to ceiling. The light was spilling into every crevice in the walls, erasing every shadow.

She opened her eyes. The cavern was bright as day. Overhead, stalactites dangled from the ceiling. White crystals sparkled along the walls. Belial was gone – at least for now. Somehow, she knew she hadn't seen the last of him.

The light from the cavern poured into the tunnel behind her. She ran along the tunnel, and hoped it wasn't too late to catch up with Nissa and Mica. She contacted Nissa by thought.

"We're in some kind of dungeon," Nissa replied. "One of the Egoz has gone back to look for you."

Already, Enna could hear footsteps approaching. She turned and raced back to the cavern. The room had grown dark once more. She found a large black rock at the far end of the room and hid behind it.

The footsteps entered the cavern and stopped. The Egoz was sniffing the air like a wild animal. With a grunt, he began inspecting the room.

Enna could smell him before she could see him. There was a putrid, revolting air about the Egoz, and she held her breath. She watched his legs as he passed by the black rock where she was hiding. His pants were worn and torn around the ankles, his bare feet blackened from the cave floors.

With a dissatisfied grunt, the Egoz left the cavern. Enna slipped from her hiding place and followed. She expected him to lead her to the dungeon where Nissa and Mica were being held, and that is precisely what he did.

At the end of the tunnel, a ladder leaned against the wall, leading to a chamber below. Enna watched from around a corner as the Egoz descended the ladder.

Enna crept toward the ladder and peered into the lower chamber. Along the walls, hanging crystals were alight like lanterns, casting a soft white glow over the room. Nissa was standing against one wall. Two Egoz stood before her, grunting and gesturing wildly with their arms.

Nissa sensed Enna's presence, but she didn't dare look up. She was watching the Egoz with wide, frightened eyes, cringing each time they moved toward her.

"They're trying to communicate with me," Nissa thought to Enna. "I think they're interested in the furniture in our first prison cell – the chairs, the tables, the pictures. They want to know how we created it. I think it's been a while since they've been able to create anything like that."

"How *did* you create it?" Enna wondered.

"I don't have a clue! When we were tossed into that prison, a comfortable living room was the furthest thing from my mind."

"Not for me," Mica thought from inside a wire cage in the corner of the room. "I was thinking, if we're trapped here anyway… wouldn't it be nice if there was some place soft and warm where I could take my next nap."

"Don't worry. I'll get you out," Enna promised. But before she could determine when or how, strong, thin arms wrapped around her waist. She gasped, flailing in her captor's grasp. He released her suddenly, and she dropped to the dungeon floor like a stone.

Nissa raced to her side. "Are you OK?"

Enna just nodded, staring up at the Egoz who had

seized her. He, in turn, was staring down at her with vacant, expressionless eyes.

*What would the Egoz do now?* Enna wondered. Time seemed to stop as Enna waited for the Egoz' next move. Much to her surprise, all of the Egoz simply left the dungeon, bolting the trapdoor behind them.

Nissa helped Enna to her feet. Then, from somewhere in the dungeon, Enna heard weeping. She glanced around. In the corner of the room, a small elf crouched, her face buried in her hands.

"Who is it?"

The elf raised her head, her cheeks streaked with tears.

"Ellie! What are you doing here?"

"I couldn't find my way back to the village," Ellie replied between sobs. "So I decided to follow you. But you were already way ahead of me and I couldn't catch up."

"No one from Geter's rescue team saw you?"

Ellie shook her head. "No one saw me until I got into the caves, and then the Egoz found me. They took me straight to this dungeon, and I've been here for hours."

"Was it you who called to us for help?" Enna wondered.

"Yes, but you didn't help me," Ellie replied bitterly.

"Well, we're here now," Nissa thought dryly. "To the rescue."

"You can't help me! You're a prisoner just like me." Ellie glared up at Enna and Nissa.

"That will teach you to mind your own business," Nissa started, but Enna shook her head. This was no time for lectures.

"Ahem," Mica thought from the corner of the room. "Over here. Large cat trapped in a small cage."

Enna peeked at Mica through his boxy wire cage.

"Let my freedom be your first priority," he suggested.

Enna worked at untangling the chains on Mica's cage, while Nissa scoured the dungeon walls for a way out.

At last, Mica's cage door swung open and he pushed through the small doorway. Once free, he stretched his legs and rolled on to his side.

"Much better," he thought, purring contentedly.

"How can you be happy, Mica?" Nissa sighed, still feeling her way along the walls. "We're locked in a dungeon far beneath the earth. And since we can't communicate with the Egoz about how we created all that lovely furniture, they'll realize they have no use for us. Then they'll just leave us here."

"Right," Mica thought distractedly, sniffing the bags of food at his sides. "That *is* bad. Grab me a cat treat, will you?"

"You're all out," Enna replied.

Immediately, Mica got to his feet and paced the floor restlessly. "This is ridiculous," he thought. "We have got to get out of here."

Nissa just rolled her eyes.

An hour later, Enna, Nissa and Ellie were sitting three in a row against the dungeon wall, staring at the wall opposite them. Ellie's sobbing had stopped, her tear ducts finally dry. Now she just scowled miserably at anyone who glanced in her direction.

Enna and Nissa had tried contacting Grandmother, but

they weren't able to get through. Something was blocking their thoughts.

"You realize we're no further ahead than when we first entered the crystal caves," Nissa sighed, shifting her head to stare up at the ceiling for a change of scenery. "We still have no idea where Gael is, if she's even still here in the Egoz' caves."

"I saw Gael," Ellie thought.

Enna and Nissa stared at her in surprise.

"You've seen Gael? Why didn't you mention it before?" Nissa demanded.

"Well, sorry if I'm not thinking about Gael at the moment," Ellie replied sarcastically.

"But that's why we're here," Nissa thought, trying to control her outrage. "To save Gael."

"It's not why I'm here," Ellie replied stiffly, shifting uncomfortably on the floor.

"You are just unbelievable," Nissa burst, her face flushing with anger.

"Not now," Enna thought, grasping Nissa's hand.

"Not all of us can be heroes, I guess," Ellie added haughtily. "Not that you're doing a very good job of that, either."

"Where did you see Gael?" Enna asked quickly before Nissa could reply.

"In a chamber not far from here. I saw her when the Egoz brought me here."

"Was she OK?"

"I don't know. I just saw her lying on a cot. She wasn't moving." Ellie lowered her eyes and studied her hands in her lap.

Enna felt a huge knot in her throat. “When?”

“A few hours ago.”

“Maybe she’s still there,” Enna thought, turning to Nissa.

“Not that it matters,” Nissa replied. “We’re still stuck in here.”

They returned to staring at the wall opposite them. Another hour passed, then another. All the while, Enna found her thoughts returning to Elffolk. She was remembering the oddest things. In her mind, she could hear her grandfather’s rocking chair on her front porch, where he smoked his pipe before bedtime. When she closed her eyes, she could see every last line in her grandmother’s face. Those lines, those rocking chair creaks had never meant a thing before that day. Yet, now that there was a chance she’d never see or hear those things again, they meant the whole world.

For as long as Enna could remember, she had longed to explore the world beyond the imaginary line. She was bored of the village’s routines and simplicity, tired of the same trees, buildings and elves. She dreamed of faraway places and imagined a magical world just over the mountains. But now, for the first time in her life, she could think of nothing better than being home. Suddenly, home seemed like the most magical place on earth.

Just then, a thought occurred to Enna. “Have we learned nothing?” she questioned, sitting up straight.

“What were we supposed to learn?” Nissa asked tiredly. “Not to hang around in dark caves? Not to chase after creatures whose eyes glow in the dark? No offence, Mica.”

"None taken," Mica replied, raising his head a fraction of an inch. He'd been fast asleep for the past three hours. "Are we free yet?"

"No," Nissa replied in a huff.

"All righty. Wake me when we're free and all is well." With that, Mica laid down his head and fell asleep.

"What I'm trying to say," Enna continued, "is that we're in the crystal caves, where anything is possible, remember? We just have to imagine it, feel it and believe it. And here we are, feeling sorry for ourselves."

"You're right," Nissa thought. "We have to believe that we'll be freed."

But another hour passed and Enna, Nissa, Ellie and Mica were still trapped in the Egoz' dungeon.

"Why isn't it working?" Ellie demanded.

"Don't give up," Enna thought. "We have to stay focused."

Above them the trapdoor swung open and an Egoz peered into the prison cell. With a grunt, he motioned for them to follow.

## — CHAPTER TWELVE —

# *Swept Away*

The Egoz led Enna, Nissa, Ellie and Mica through a complicated series of tunnels. Each tunnel looked the same as the one before, and Enna wondered how the Egoz didn't get lost in the caves. Finally, they passed by a glowing chamber, white light spilling on to the tunnel floor in front of them.

Enna felt a tug at her sleeve.

"That's where I saw her," Ellie thought. "Gael was in there."

Enna glanced up at the tall, willowy Egoz whose thin, bony fingers were wrapped around her arm. She craned her neck to peer into the chamber as she passed by. The glowing lights were blindingly bright and her eyes shut automatically.

"Gael," she thought desperately. "Tell me if you're in there!"

There was no reply.

Enna yanked her arm away, breaking free from her surprised captor. She turned and sprinted toward the glowing chamber.

"Enna!" Nissa called after her. "Where are you going?"

All communication ceased the instant Enna entered the glowing room. She waited for her eyes to adjust to the bright light. Slowly, she was able to make sense of the shapes in the room. She was surrounded by crystals – huge crystals that rose all the way to the thirty-foot ceiling.

The door to the room slammed shut behind her. She raced to the door and pushed. It was locked. She was trapped.

As her vision adjusted, she realized the source of the glowing lights. Dozens of holograms were flickering throughout the room. Memories from the crystals were moving all around her. Some were so faint they were perfectly transparent; others were so strong they seemed almost real.

In one of the holograms, a huge creature like the one that had tried to trample her was casually grazing on plants. In another hologram, seven or eight big people were sitting around a table. Then one slammed a fist on to the table and stormed off. In yet another hologram, a tall woman held a baby in her arms. She was looking up to the sky, a horrified expression on her face. A second later, she raced out of view.

Images of big people surrounded Enna. She stared in awe, her mouth dropped open. She had never fully believed the tales of the dreaded big people. She had always assumed the stories were mythical. But now, she was seeing the big people with her very own eyes.

Enna watched the holograms, her eyes moving from one to the next. She heard the sounds of falling rain and howling wind. She heard shouts and cries, as well as laughter and singing. Everywhere she turned, new images were forming, others fading away. The place was teeming with memories of things long forgotten.

She found herself growing more and more exhausted. The sounds and sights were overwhelming. She covered her ears and shut her eyes, but she couldn't drown out the noises and flashing lights.

"Make it stop," she thought. "Nissa! Help me!"

Somehow, she knew that Nissa wouldn't be able to receive her thoughts. The memories were interfering.

Enna moved to a corner of the room and curled into a ball, trying to block out the lights and sounds. "Nissa, you have to save me," she thought.

She glanced up just once, hoping to see Nissa at the door to the chamber. Instead, she spotted a hologram, a memory, of Gael. Gael was lying on a cot, carried by two Egoz. The Egoz set her down on the ground, but she didn't move.

Enna walked to the spot on the floor where the hologram of Gael flickered. As the minutes passed by and Gael still didn't stir, Enna's heart sank. Perhaps Gael was dead. Enna sucked in a sharp breath and tried to hold back her tears.

*Gael, please get up,* Enna thought to herself.

Slowly, the hologram Gael moved. She lifted a hand and felt her head. She eased herself up to a sitting position and sat on the cot, gathering her strength. Then she got up and walked around, examining the very room in which Enna now stood.

*She was here,* Enna thought happily. *She's alive!* Hot tears of relief flowed down Enna's cheeks. But her relief quickly faded as the holograms continued to bombard her with memories. She returned to her corner and held her knees to her chest.

"Please hurry, Nissa," Enna thought. She didn't know how long she'd last in this place before losing her mind.

She had no idea how much time had already passed. Recent and ancient memories blurred together, some lasting just a few seconds, others continuing on and on, distorting all sense of time.

Enna curled into a ball on the floor once again and closed her eyes.

"Enna!"

Despite Enna's best efforts, she couldn't block out the sounds.

"Enna! Up here!"

Weakly, Enna opened her eyes and glanced up. Nissa was waving at her about halfway up the wall. But Enna had seen so much already, her brain didn't process the image. *Just another hologram,* Enna thought to herself and covered her eyes with her arm.

Enna felt her arms lift. Someone was pulling her up. Gradually, she rose to her feet.

"Enna, look at me. Focus!"

Slowly, Nissa's face came into view. "Nissa, is it really you?" Enna asked uncertainly.

"Yes, really me."

"But how?"

"There's a tunnel, up there." Nissa pointed to the wall.

"You probably didn't even notice it with all the images around you. But you'll have to climb. Are you up for it?"

Enna nodded tiredly.

"OK, I'll give you a boost up."

Wearily, Enna climbed, clinging to the rough rocks and smooth crystals lining the wall. Finally, she reached a narrow ledge and stared into a long, dark tunnel. A minute later, Nissa joined her on the ledge.

"Nissa, you crawled through there all by yourself?"

Nissa nodded. "I'll go first. You follow me."

"But Nissa," Enna protested weakly, looking at her sister in surprise. "You never go first."

Nissa grinned at her. "Just follow me, OK?"

As Enna distanced herself from the glowing room, her strength returned. The tunnel sloped downwards and emptied into a chamber. Climbing out of the tunnel, Enna spotted Ellie against the far wall. Mica was back in his cage, a glum look on his face.

"You all right?" Mica asked.

"I'll be OK," Enna thought. She glanced around at their new prison cell. "I see we're still trapped."

"Some more than others," Mica replied unhappily.

"I'll get you out of your cage," Enna thought. As Enna worked at the rusty chains on Mica's cage, she told the others about the hologram of Gael.

"That's the first bit of good news I've heard all day," Nissa thought.

"Now we just have to find her and save her," Enna nodded.

"And how do you think you're going to do that when, once again, we're trapped as well?" Ellie asked impatiently.

Ellie had a point, but Enna and Nissa chose to ignore her.

Finally, Enna untangled the chains on Mica's cage, and Mica burst through the cage door. He stretched his limbs and brushed against Enna in gratitude.

"Why do they keep putting *me* in a cage, anyway?" Mica asked.

"Because they're most afraid of you," Enna replied kindly.

"Well, that's probably true," he thought. "Say, do you think they're going to feed us in here?"

"I doubt it," Ellie scoffed.

"Right," Mica thought. "Well, that's too bad. I could really go for some fresh fish right about now. A bird maybe. Duck would be superb – wouldn't that be delicious?" He searched the floor around him hungrily. "Oh heck, I'd eat a cricket right now."

All of a sudden, the door to their prison cell creaked open. Two Egoz appeared at the doorway and motioned for them to come.

Again the prisoners were led through a series of winding, forking tunnels. They arrived at a huge chamber. Tall pointed crystals lined the walls and a soft white glow filled the room. At the far end of the room, they could just make out a tall stone chair.

The Egoz pushed the elves and Mica ahead of them. Uncertainly, they shuffled forwards. As they approached the chair, they realized an Egoz was seated on it. With grey skin, he nearly blended right into the stone.

The elves stopped several yards before the chair,

understanding that they were finally meeting the leader of the Egoz. The Egoz shifted in his chair and beckoned the elves forward with a finger.

Enna took a few more steps, and quickly realized she was the only one who had moved. The leader of the Egoz stared at Enna curiously and motioned for her to come closer still.

Her heart pounding in her chest, Enna approached the chair and looked into the Egoz' face. There was something different about this one.

Then she spotted something in his lap. It was the picture of the white city that she had seen above the mantle in the first dungeon.

The Egoz' long, thin fingers were wrapped around the edges of the frame and he stared at the picture a long time. Finally, he glanced up at Enna.

"Do you know this place?" he asked.

Startled, Enna stumbled backwards. "I'm sorry," she thought quickly. "It's just I didn't realize you could communicate telepathically."

"I'm the only one who can. The only one who still remembers," he replied and glanced down at the picture again. "We found this in the dungeon where you were staying."

"I don't know the place," Enna thought. "I've never seen it before."

"It's so familiar," the Egoz replied. "And yet, I can't place it."

Though his expression hardly changed, Enna could have sworn he looked sad. She wondered whether he was remembering his former life as an elf, before he'd become an Egoz.

"It's beautiful," Enna added.

The Egoz looked into Enna's eyes. "Yes, it is."

"Please, we've just come to save Gael," Enna thought. "If you would release her, we'll all go home, never to bother you again."

The leader of the Egoz looked at the picture in his lap once again. A long time passed before he raised his head. "Will you find this place and tell me where it is?"

Enna swallowed hard, staring at the picture of the white city. "Yes."

"OK," the leader replied. With that, he stood up from his chair and spoke to his guards at the back of the room with grunts, squawks and howls. The guards rushed forward, seizing the elves at once.

Enna turned back to the leader. "Where are they taking us?"

The leader of the Egoz just sat back down on his chair and watched his prisoners leave.

Winding through the dark caves, Enna wondered what the Egoz had in store for them next. Did yet another dark dungeon await them, or were they finally being freed?

They found themselves back in the cavern where they had first encountered the glowing green eyes of the Egoz. And there, in the centre of the room, was Gael. An expression of relief poured over her face when she spotted them.

"Thank the great spirits," she thought, pulling everyone all at once into a sloppy embrace.

"You're OK?" Enna asked. Gael didn't appear the slightest bit hurt.

"Bump to the shoulder and head, but it cleared up quickly," Gael replied, beaming at the elves and Mica in turn.

"What happened?" Nissa asked.

"The Egoz agreed to release me," Gael answered.

"But why?" Nissa asked.

"I suspect that has something to do with you elves," Gael thought with a smile.

"The white city," Enna thought. "The leader of the Egoz asked me to find the city in the picture, and I agreed to do it."

"Very courageous of you," Gael praised. Glancing at the Egoz still in the room, she handed Enna's pack and lantern to her. "Here are your things," she thought, pulling her own satchel over her shoulder. Gently, she pushed everyone toward the exit. "This way now, and quickly. Before they change their minds."

The freed prisoners rushed through the tunnel.

"I'm sorry we weren't able to communicate. The holograms in the Egoz' caves interfere with our thoughts," Gael explained.

"Why did you come to the crystal caves?" Nissa asked Gael as they moved through the tunnel.

"I came to the crystal caves to learn of a prophecy."

"A prophecy?" Enna asked.

"A prediction."

"So what was the prediction?" Nissa prompted.

"A story for another day," Gael replied. She spotted

Nissa's confused expression. "It's a long story, really."

"Why did the Egoz take you prisoner?" Enna wondered.

"So many questions," Gael thought. "I promise I'll tell you everything. But for now, let's just keep moving."

Suddenly, Gael stopped in her tracks, a look of alarm on her face. "Do you hear it?"

Enna just shook her head. She hadn't heard any – oh, there it was – a low rumbling sound. Whatever it was, it was growing louder by the second.

"The Egoz have opened up the underground river," Gael thought. "They want to get rid of us once and for all. We're being flushed out of the caves!"

Frozen on the spot, Enna, Nissa, Ellie and Mica just stared at each other.

"Well, don't just stand there," Gael thought. "Run!"

Then the elves were running, their feet pounding against the ground, their hearts racing wildly. Mica passed them on the left and took the lead.

Up ahead, the tunnel forked.

"Which way?" Nissa thought desperately.

Out of nothing, Kaya appeared in the tunnel to the right. "This way."

The rumbling sound had become a deafening roar. Enna glanced back just once. Water splashed around a corner in the tunnel behind her. All at once, a wall of water was rushing toward her.

Just before the water reached her, Enna drew a deep breath and closed her eyes. With an incredible force, the water washed her through the tunnel. She was tumbling, rolling and somersaulting. Then she was falling. With arms and legs flailing, she dropped down and down, and it seemed very possible that she'd just been tossed off the end of the earth.

At last, she splashed into a pool of cold water. Sinking to the bottom of the pond like a pebble, she looked up. Even through the water, she could see that the sky was alight with twinkling stars. She knew she was out of the crystal caves. Yet, she couldn't find the strength to swim to the surface.

The last of her breath escaped her lips in bubbles. She watched the bubbles rise to the surface of the pond. If only she could reach the surface, too. But it seemed so very far away.

In short, clipped images, memories from her life flashed before her. Long forgotten memories returned in a rush. Her life in Elffolk unfolded in her mind.

She was a baby glancing around her sun-filled home for the very first time. She was holding her grandmother's hand, trying her very best to climb the village steps. She was held high in the air by two strong arms, giggling and staring down into the smiling face of someone she couldn't quite place.

The images continued until Enna was reliving the moment when she had dropped from the crystal caves, splashed into the pond and sank to the bottom. Then the images stopped.

She glanced up again to the still surface of the pond. The stars were flickering in the night sky. The full moon was shining brightly.

Just before she closed her eyes for the very last time,

she spotted something above her. A small hand was reaching into the water.

Nissa lifted Enna to the surface of the pond. With Gael's help, she dragged Enna up on to the rocky shore.

"You all right?" Nissa asked, her large brown eyes larger than ever as she peered down at Enna.

Enna coughed and sputtered a few times, turning her face to the side. She nodded weakly. "Is everyone else OK?"

"They're fine."

"Where's Mica?"

Nissa pointed, trying to hold back a grin. "He's a little upset right now."

Upset only began to describe the expression on Mica's face, as water dripped from his chin, wet fur clinging to his body. He was shivering, uncomfortable and undignified. He glanced at Enna sourly.

Enna couldn't help but laugh. "Oh Mica, you're so much thinner than I would have thought! I had no idea you were mostly fur."

"Very funny," Mica replied bitterly, turning his wet face the other way.

Enna glanced down at her hands and arms and smiled to herself. The mud from the quicksand was gone at last. She was clean.

— CHAPTER THIRTEEN —

# *Celebration and Secrecy*

The group had been flushed from the crystal caves into a valley east of Elffolk.

Gael led the elves through the woods, their hair and clothing drenched and dripping. Shivering in the cool night air, they longed only for dry clothes and a warm fireplace.

Enna contacted her grandparents, and they agreed to meet in the village square.

As they trudged through the forest, the stars faded overhead. An orange glow warmed the horizon behind them. Dawn had broken. The day and night that never seemed to end had come to an end at last.

Ellie trailed a few yards behind the others. With arms folded across her chest, she scowled at Enna and Nissa every time they glanced behind them.

"I'm cold," Ellie thought bitterly, narrowing her eyes at Enna. "And it's your fault."

"My fault?" Enna replied in surprise. "How is it my fault?"

"I wouldn't be here if it wasn't for you."

"It was your choice to follow us into the forest."

"Yes, but – "

"No one even asked you to follow us," Enna added.

"Still," Ellie replied stubbornly, "if you hadn't gone against Geter's orders and taken it upon yourselves to save the day, I wouldn't have had to follow you. And then I wouldn't be wet and I wouldn't be freezing!"

Nissa shook her head angrily. In fact, she looked about ready to boil over. Enna just sighed. There was no point trying to reason with Ellie.

"Are we almost there?" Ellie asked again, the fifth time since leaving the crystal caves.

"Elffolk is just ahead," Gael thought calmly.

"How come we can't see it?"

"The members of the high council spend a great deal of time making sure that it remains invisible – invisible to anyone beyond the imaginary line," Gael explained.

The elves looked confused.

"Everything is made up of energy, and energy vibrates. The elves of the high council work to raise the vibration of the village – meaning they work to make it vibrate faster. At a certain level of vibration, the village moves into the next dimension. So that means a stranger could pass by Elffolk and not even see it."

She met confused faces all around.

"This higher vibration only goes as far as the imaginary line," Gael added.

"So, is that why we're not supposed to go beyond the imaginary line?" Enna asked.

"Right, the protection ends past the line."

By the time they had reached the outskirts of

Elffolk, the sun was shining and their clothes were dry. Somewhere, they had crossed the imaginary line, because they could see grey smoke rising from the chimneys in the village. The round, stone homes came into view. A handful of stray chickens and two village goats wandered the pathways between the buildings. And all around them birds were singing.

They breathed in the familiar smell of pine trees and burning logs.

These were the very same sights, sounds and smells that greeted them each and every morning. Yet, on this particular morning, those sights, sounds and smells were never more welcomed.

"Sometimes it takes going away, or nearly losing it all, to appreciate what we already have," Gael thought to Enna.

Waiting in the village square were Grandmother and Grandfather, Ellie's mother, Geter, Seth and the medicine elf.

Enna and Nissa raced toward their grandparents, flinging themselves into their outstretched arms. The strained, worried expressions on their grandparents' faces vanished, and delighted smiles took over.

"Thank the great spirits," Grandmother thought. "You made it back in one piece, and you saved Gael."

Enna watched Ellie reunite with her mother. Melting into her mother's embrace, Ellie sobbed like an hysterical baby.

Then Ellie turned to Enna and Nissa, the same familiar scowl painted on her face. A moment later, Ellie's mother glanced over at Enna and matched her daughter's scornful expression.

Enna just sighed. Some elves learn nothing.

The laughter and merriment in the village square roused the other villagers. Soon sleepy, curious elves were peering from their doors and windows.

When the villagers spotted Gael and the rescue team, they poured out of their homes to the square. Some didn't even bother to change from their night clothes. When a number of villagers had gathered, Geter climbed on to his box in the centre of the square and officially announced the safe return of Gael, Enna, Nissa and Ellie.

"Mica, too," Enna added.

"And who could forget our fearless feline friend," Geter added smoothly as if it hadn't been an oversight. All eyes turned to Mica who was sitting tall next to Geter. Mica held his head a little higher, graciously accepting the many thoughts of praise.

Geter droned on for several minutes more, until Gael yanked him off his box, to the cheers and laughter of the audience. She climbed on to the box herself and addressed the audience.

"Thank you all for your good thoughts and wishes. Thank you to Enna, Nissa and Mica for their tremendous courage and persistence. If not for them, I would not be standing here now."

"Tell us what happened!" one of the elves thought.

"Tell us everything!"

"From the very beginning!"

Gael peered down at those gathered around her. The

elves loved a good story, and all faces were rapt with interest.

"I go to the black cliffs from time to time, as many of you were not aware," Gael began. "Inside the cliffs are caves filled with thousands and thousands of crystals. The crystals hold many memories and offer many powers. I went to the caves to learn of a prophecy, which I will explain in detail another time."

The elves glanced at one another curiously.

"I was inside a crystal cave when the earthquake struck," Gael continued. "The earthquake loosened the rocks and crystals in the cave and they came tumbling down around me. I didn't have time to escape. One rock hit me on the shoulder and knocked me to the ground. Another hit my head and everything went black.

"I lay unconscious on the cold, stone floor, pinned to the ground with a heavy rock on my chest. Even in my deep sleep, I felt the burden of this rock and knew that I was trapped. Then the weight lifted. Slowly, I opened my eyes and found myself staring into a face with grey skin and glowing green eyes. I glanced around and saw that we were not alone. Five or six more of these creatures surrounded me."

"What were they?" someone asked Gael.

"They were the Egoz," Gael replied. "Creatures who have made their home in the crystal caves. They keep to themselves, never leaving the caves. And they don't like visitors.

"The Egoz captured me and brought me back to their caves. They wanted my help in ridding them of a powerful dark force that has invaded their caves. This dark force seeks power more than anything else, and he wants to rule the Egoz."

"Belial," Enna thought and Nissa nodded.

"In all my years, I've never met anything like this dark force," Gael thought, shaking her head. "His power is greater than anything I've ever known. He feeds on the dark energies around him – greed, fear, jealousy, despair. So, he is growing more powerful all the time. He caused that last earthquake. And he's bent on more destruction."

"Can he be stopped?"

"He must be stopped," Gael thought gravely. "Unfortunately, I don't know how, and I wasn't able to help the Egoz."

Enna shivered. She had a strong suspicion she'd be seeing Belial again.

"While a prisoner, I learned that the Egoz had also captured Nissa, Enna, Ellie and Mica," Gael thought. "However, the Egoz refused to let any of us go. It wasn't until the leader communicated with Enna, and Enna agreed to help him, that he released us."

All eyes turned to Enna.

"What did you agree to do?" someone asked.

"To find the white city," Enna replied.

There was a buzz among the elves in the crowd as they turned to one another and exchanged thoughts, and Enna wondered whether the elves had heard of the city.

"What about the prophecy?" one of the older elves asked Gael. "What did it say?"

"All in good time, all in good time," Gael thought,

attempting to lift the mood. "We have returned safely. We are home among friends and family once again. Now is the time to celebrate!"

The crowd clapped and cheered.

"But it's barely past dawn," someone protested tiredly.

"What better time?"

With that the elves got to work, readying the village square for the festivities. Two elves hauled a wooden table to the square. Two more carried fresh, steaming loaves of bread from the bakery and set them on the table. A flutist began playing a lively tune. And a handful of elves danced as if they hadn't just rolled out of bed minutes before.

Mica was still standing in the centre of the square. He was soaking up the attention and pats from passing elves.

"So, how did you get past the dark magic?" Geter asked Enna. She turned to glance up at him. He was being friendly, but he was genuinely curious, too.

"There is no dark magic, after all. It's just the crystals magnifying our own thoughts and feelings."

"And the king of the crystal caves?" Geter asked. "How is he?"

"You know about him?"

Geter raised an eyebrow and smiled knowingly.

"He's very well," Enna thought with a laugh.

Just then, Grandmother wrapped her arms around Enna and Nissa. "My brave elves," she thought with a warm smile.

"You wouldn't believe all the crystals we saw," Nissa thought. She went on to describe the crystals, the way they poked through the ground, the way they jutted from the black cliffs at precarious angles.

Enna opened her pack and retrieved the crystal she'd collected. She handed it over as Grandmother's eyes grew big.

"It's beautiful," Grandmother remarked, examining it from all angles. "It holds many memories."

Enna was reminded of the holograms she'd seen in the crystal caves. She wondered how many other periods of history – and lives – were remembered there. Had their own adventures been captured by the crystals – to be viewed ages and ages hence?

The medicine elf approached Enna and Nissa, inviting them to step into his office.

"We're fine!" Nissa insisted, but the medicine elf was more insistent. Reluctantly, they followed him back to his office. He cleaned and bandaged their scraped knees and hands, checked their eyes and ears, and tested their reflexes. Satisfied that they were perfectly healthy, he sent them back to the party.

When Enna and Nissa returned to the village square, Gael was nowhere in sight. Ellie was gone, too. Even Mica had slipped away – the idea of food or a good long nap finally coaxing him off. Yet, the party was carrying on as before. It didn't seem to matter that those being celebrated were not actually in attendance. The elves were always looking for an excuse to party.

Enna searched the crowd for Gael. "Where do you think she went?" she asked Nissa.

Nissa just shrugged. "She can't be far."

It was true. Not far away, but just out of sight, Gael was emptying her satchel. The old scroll that Kaya had given her tumbled to the ground. Carefully, Gael picked it up and unrolled it. Wet from the underground river, the symbols on the scroll were barely visible.

Gael could not have read the symbols on the scroll, anyway, but she knew what they had said. They said that their island – Atlantis – would be shaken and lost to the seas. She didn't know when it would happen. Perhaps it was still far off. Perhaps there was still a chance that they could save Atlantis.

Gael would not let herself fall into despair. Even if the prophecy were true, and the world as they knew it was about to change, it did not mean that all would be lost. Change would bring hardship – especially to those who resisted it – but it would bring new opportunities, too. After all, life is change. It is the only thing to be counted on for certain.

Gael would have to share the prophecy with the elves. The only question was when. But as she gazed back to the village square, and spotted the happy faces and heard their laughter, she thought to herself, now is not the time.

*Now is the time to be joyful.*

## *Acknowledgments*

To my husband Vlad for his love, support and wonderful company; my mom for inspiring me, believing in me and reading all the drafts; my dad just for being a terrific dad; Teresa de Grosbois for her guidance and encouragement; Janet Glasspool for her careful edits and thoughtful suggestions; William Stockmann for bringing the images in my mind to life through his artwork; Becky Blue, Vicki Eldstrom, Rae and Fiona Fox, David Furlong, Jeremy Hiebert, Lisa Kathleen, Adrienne Price, Anna-Mae Sebastian and Laura Slauson for their helpful reviews; and finally Karl the cat who is the inspiration for "Mica."

*About the Author*

Tina McFadden's writing career began at age six. By age nine, she had written a whole series of mystery novels.

A full-time writer and editor, Tina has published articles in magazines, newspapers and on the web, as well as short fictional stories for children and adults. *Elffolk and the Crystal Caves of Atlantis* is her first published novel.

Tina was born in British Columbia, grew up in Ontario and currently resides in Calgary, Alberta with her husband Vlad. When she's not writing about the adventures of fictional characters, she enjoys real-life adventures like hiking in the mountains and travelling abroad.

Visit www.elffolk.com.